Updraft

Updraft

*It was silly to worry about a piece of paper flying over
the Atlantic on the edges of a storm.*

SANDRA FINLEY DORAN

Pacific Press®
Publishing Association
Nampa, Idaho | www.pacificpress.com

Hart Research Center

Cover design: Tamara Slocum
Cover resources: GettyImages.com
Interior design: Aaron Troia

Copyright © 2023 by Hart Research®
Published by Pacific Press® Publishing Association in agreement
    with Hart Research Center
Printed in the United States of America
All rights reserved

The author assumes full responsibility for the accuracy of all facts and
quotations as cited in this book.

Unless otherwise noted, all Scripture quotations are from the New King
James Version®. Copyright © 1982 by Thomas Nelson. Used by permission. All rights reserved.

Scripture quotations marked KJV are from the King James Version.

Scripture quotations marked NIV are from THE HOLY BIBLE, NEW
INTERNATIONAL VERSION®. Copyright © 1973, 1978, 1984,
2011 by Biblica, Inc.® Used by permission. All rights reserved world-
wide.

To order additional copies of this book, call toll-free
1-800-765-6955 or visit http://www.adventistbookcenter.com.

ISBN 978-0-8163-6912-6

January 2023

Preface

It has been my lifelong passion to share the amazing message of Revelation's three angels streaming through the heavens to alert men and women of the events that will take place before Jesus comes. This book approaches the topic in a unique manner. But the method is not new. Thousands of years ago, Jesus stirred the hearts of his listeners by crafting his messages in authentic scenes familiar to their everyday life. Whether they listened to stories of lost coins, wandering sheep, or scattered seeds, people took notice of the deeper truths embedded in familiar scenes.

Similarly, the book you hold in your hands has been written to captivate the interest of readers in the twenty-first century. Intertwining the lives and struggles of very different characters, the story is also an entry point to pique interest for further study into Revelation 14. This book is just your first step. Whether you are a Bible scholar or a baby Christian, this story is intended to whet your appetite for further study of the three angels' messages.

Beyond that, *Updraft* is a story meant to be shared. The real power lies in what happens after you turn the last page. Enjoy the story. But don't stop there. Share it with a neighbor. Discuss it with a friend. Talk about the deeper issues at a book club. Like Alice the warrior in the pages that follow, pray for courage and keep the momentum going!

Dan Houghton,
executive director, *Three Angels for Kids*;
president, *Hart Research Center*

One

Alice Jones was a worrier. Not a warrior, her husband, Lance, had loved to remind her—a worrier. Alice figured that if she did the worrying, no one else would have to. It was the least she could for people. She had worried when Lance developed a spot on his lung. Worried when the doctors said they must remove it. Worried when the biopsy showed cancer. Worried every day until Lance breathed his last.

But the funny thing was, once there was nothing left to do, Alice stopped worrying about her own life. After all, why worry about your situation when the thing you had feared most has already happened?

It was not like she didn't miss Lance. She felt his absence like a big hole in her heart. She thought about him every day. His warm hand in hers at church. His baritone voice.

His gentle prayers. But of course, there was no longer any need to worry. Lance was sleeping now, waiting for Jesus to come.

So Alice turned her worries to a new cause: the people around her. She worried about the child in the park with the perpetually runny nose. The mailman with a limp. The couple that argued. The scowling runner.

"We have to find a way to help them," she begged her pastor. "Everything they need is in the Bible. But how do we get them to sit up and take notice?"

Pastor Vic agreed wholeheartedly. But the best plan of action was yet to be determined. So they met every Monday and prayed, asking God to write the script.

On the Tuesday morning after Labor Day, Alice awoke with a start. The three angels' messages. That was it. That was what they needed. The thought was so clear in her head, she felt like she had always known it. Now that she had pulled the idea into the light of day, it was time to move into action.

Alice threw back the mauve floral bedspread, her heart pounding with a joy she had not known since losing Lance. She made the bed with a flourish, showered quickly, patted a few drops of lavender oil on her cheeks and headed for the kitchen. As she heated the water for her tea, she continued to entertain the thoughts racing through her mind.

The love of Jesus as demonstrated in the judgment, the first angel's message.

That's what the scowling runner needed. The man was obviously not happy. He ran like a person in pain, pushing himself so hard that Alice could barely handle watching him as he passed her house. He was trying too hard. Wanting to prove something. There was nothing to prove. Jesus had already proved it.

Alice hummed as she dunked her cinnamon-apple tea bag up and down three times in the cup Lance had given her last Christmas that bore the phrase *Jesus is the reason for the season*. More than that, she had told Lance—the reason for the off-season too.

Spreading almond butter on a piece of raisin toast, Alice paused. She knew what she had to do. But how would she ever get the people who needed to hear the message to the right place at the right time? *Not your problem, Alice Jones*, she reminded herself. *Walk by faith, not by sight.*

Today was a new day. She would be Alice the warrior, not Alice the worrier.

* * * * *

Pastor Vic Morales was bending over his garden, snipping a few late-blooming zinnias for his wife, Esther, when his cell phone sounded in his back pocket. He grabbed the phone, straightened up, and stuck the handful of yellow and red flowers in a bucket beside his feet.

"Alice?" He had never heard the woman's voice so high. "Is everything OK?"

"More than OK, Pastor Vic," she answered. "We have work to do. When can we meet?"

The pastor was glad Alice was not on video call. He

would have hated for her to see the look of exasperation that was crossing his face. He had just met with the woman last evening. And he had not taken a day off in three weeks. He glanced over at the shed, where his ten-speed bike was calling his name.

"Is this an emergency, Alice?"

"Depends on how you look at it, pastor." She paused, feeling a slight chill of worry creeping toward her heart. What was she worrying about? That she would lose the thought? That the pastor would not get on board? That the opportunity would be missed? That God's plan would be thwarted? *Be a warrior, Alice*, she told herself. *Not a worrier.*

"Alice?"

"Actually, it's not an emergency. In fact, let me play with a few ideas and bring them to you next Monday."

"As long as everything is OK." Pastor Vic tried not to sound too relieved, but he could almost feel his smile radiating through the air.

"I'm good. Just keep praying for me. For the project. For God's will to be done."

* * * * *

Alice slipped the cell phone into its hand-sewn pouch and slung it around her neck. Study the three angels' messages. That's what she had to do. If Revelation 14 was going to change her neighborhood, then she had better be sure she knew the messages backward and forward.

Settling into the wicker rocker on her front porch, she

reached for the Bible on the small glass table. "Then I saw another angel flying in midair, and he had the eternal gospel to proclaim to those who live on the earth—to every nation, tribe, language and people" (Revelation 14:6, NIV).

Every nation, tribe, language and people! And here she was worrying about the little Northside community nestled along the coast. *Get a grip, Alice*, she told herself. *If this message is going to go to every nation, tribe, language and people, don't you think God can handle a few streets between the bay and county park?*

She picked up her tablet, tapped on the internet icon, and typed in the phrase *number of nations in the world*. In seconds the answer popped up: 193 countries, plus Palestine and the Holy See. *The Holy See. Now there's your first clue!*

Alice smiled at the irony and typed in her next phrase: *number of isolated tribes in the world*. Her eyes fell on a search result that said, "More than one hundred uncontacted tribes exist in total isolation in the world today."

The headline startled her. She had never really thought about it. There were people actually living around the globe with no contact outside of their own little villages? No electricity? No transportation? No phones? No books? She thought about the dozens of titles filling her shelves in the living room. *This one's beyond my comprehension right now, God. Just help me here in my little corner of the world—down here in Northside.*

She checked Revelation 14:6 one more time and noted two more things to investigate. The first was the number of languages in the world. If she had to wager a guess, she figured five hundred was a good approximation. Her hand paused above the tablet's keyboard. "There are more than sixty-five hundred languages spoken in the world today," the search result said.

You've got to be kidding me! Alice stood up and gazed across her front lawn to the path winding down toward the water. More than sixty-five hundred languages. That was beyond belief!

Where to even start? Well, at least Pastor Vic spoke Spanish. Two down.

Alice picked up her tablet and typed in the last phrase: *number of people groups in the world.* This time she didn't even venture a guess. Scanning the results, she shook her head. This one was mired in controversy. What was a people group? And how did you put people in boxes like ethnicity, culture, and race? Best not to go down that road.

Alice closed the tablet and bowed her head.

Lord, it's me. Alice the warrior. I'm here for You. I want to have a tiny part in spreading the gospel to a small group of people down here in Northside. Just a little corner of the 193 countries, speaking a couple of the sixty-five hundred languages. Give me the courage. Amen.

She lifted her head just in time to see the scowling runner zipping toward the park, his mouth pasted in a tight, determined line.

Two

Cameron Stanton awoke before dawn on a crystal clear morning in Northside, unaware that he was about to start a chain of events that would radically affect the lives of total strangers. He quickly donned his fisherman's cap, packed a lunch, and headed for the dock.

Out in the channel, he caught the light southeast breeze blowing in from the bay.

The Sun Odyssey yacht glided quietly as he tacked his way toward the open ocean. A white great egret stood on the bank, silhouetted before a clump of black mangrove trees. Light waves lapped the sides of the boat, tapping out a peaceful rhythm of wind, water, and sea.

But Cameron Stanton was anything but calm. He stood in the bow of his large vessel, seemingly unaware of the pristine surroundings marking his journey from home to sea. Tanned and rugged, he cut a fine figure in khaki shorts and navy polo shirt. Small motorboats passed to the leeward side, their occupants gazing at the luxurious yacht and the capable captain who owned it.

Cameron removed his fisherman's cap and ran a hand through his dark, close-cropped hair. What to do? He did not have much time. Just a few months to make a decision. He could give in to the pressure and join the business alliance or stay independent and risk the loss of everything he owned.

The answer should be obvious. Why refuse to go along with the merger? Why swim against the tide when everyone else seemed to be riding the big wave of success?

Cameron maneuvered the catamaran into the bay, heading out toward the Atlantic. He needed time to think, to search deep in his soul and pull out the answer that would make this nagging uneasiness go away.

He wished the choice would be easier. Wasn't there a way to ride the fence, to go partway? Cameron frowned into the expanse of blue all around him. He imagined himself calling Weston Reese and saying, "I've made my decision. I'd like to be part of the alliance, but I still want my independence. I'll go along with you and get all the benefits of the business operations, but I will retain the freedom to make my own decisions."

Yeah, right. Not possible. Just not possible. It was one side or the other. There was no riding the fence with this one.

On the port side, a cabin cruiser glided by, the family waving their hellos over the water. The young boy reminded Cameron of Jay at that age. Five? Maybe six? He stood, silhouetted by the sun, his little hand enthusiastically signaling his greetings.

Jay. At seventeen, he was poised for a promising future. Just one more year of high school and then off to a top-tier college for a degree in economics. Jay had worked hard through the years. He deserved the best of everything.

Cameron felt his stomach tighten. This decision wasn't just about him. Whatever choice he made, he would drag his family along with him.

Across the bay, the winds began to pick up, dotting the blue-green waters with whitecaps. A band of cirrus clouds raced overhead, sending their feathery tails across the sky. *Cirrus clouds signal a change.* The words of an old science teacher rang in his head. *Cirrus clouds signal a change.* Was this an omen? A sign? Was he facing a change?

Cameron studied the sky for an answer. He turned back to the sea, noting the pattern of light and shadow dappling the waves. Light and dark. Dark and light. Cameron drew in a breath of sea air. He needed time to think. Time to figure this thing out once and for all. He eased the vessel into a shadowy bay and hurled the anchor overboard. A loud splash shook the air. Then all was silent.

Cameron pulled a zippered bag from the seat cushion beside him, drew out a green ink pen and a piece of printer paper, and paced to the back of the boat. Sprawling across the padded cushion of a U-shaped bench, he searched the skies for an answer.

What were you supposed to do when faced with a difficult decision? Columns, he remembered. Two columns—one for pros and one for cons.

Pulling the pen down the middle of the page, Cameron concentrated on the details of the preceding weeks. First, the facts. Next, the fine points. Then the pros and cons.

Cameron chewed on the end of the pen, reflecting on the whole giant mess. The minute he had opened the email from Weston Reese, he realized his life was about to be turned upside down. Weston had been hinting at the merger for months. When he showed up at the office last week, he wasted no time in laying all the cards on the table. Facing Cameron with steely eyes, he delivered his message. All of the freight companies were in. Cameron had two choices. Join the party or find himself on the fringes, waiting for his business to dry up.

Why did life have to be so complicated? Cameron propped his paper on the back of a life vest, his pen poised. But he was not yet ready to write. Just two freight companies dominated the entire southwest region. Stanton and Reese held the reins that pulled in all the business and padded their pockets with money like fall leaves in New England. But any similarity between Cameron Stanton and Weston Reese ended there.

Through the years, Cameron had heard more stories than he could count. Reese and his partner were ruthless leaders. Their employees desperately needed the work, so they stayed on, hanging tight in poor working conditions with minimal pay and no respect. Pressing on in warehouses with relentless work orders and demanding supervisors, they did what they had to do to barely feed their families.

And somehow Reese got away with it. There had been attempts at filing cases through the years, but nothing ever came of it. Everybody knew that. And if you dared speak up, your days were numbered.

Cameron watched as a gull winged its way overhead, squawking its urgent message across the sky. The bird swooped and dipped, finding its way alone. Something inside Cameron envied the gull. The bird flew where it wished and took orders from no one. Cameron's thoughts continued to flow, weighing the options. All he wanted to do was live up to his own ideals. Treat people with dignity. Pay them what they were worth.

Ideals? It had been years since he had stepped into a church, but he remembered the deep principles he had learned as a child. Dressed in a little blue suit, he had stood before the people of the Dayville Central Church and recited the text by memory: "So in everything, do to others what you would have them do to you, for this sums up the Law and the Prophets" (Matthew 7:12, NIV).

Church? When had he stopped going? What had changed?

Cameron straightened up. This was not the time to go down that road. He had enough to figure out. He gripped the pen tightly and began to write in green ink, filling the pro column with thoughts that flowed from him like a rushing stream.

Goodwill with colleagues.
Guaranteed steady income.
Likely increase in revenue.
Secure future for Jay.

He paused for a moment. Marilyn. Cameron drew in a huge breath of briny air.

Marilyn. He may as well just add the word *Marilyn* to the list. No other explanation needed. His wife's name said it all. If Marilyn thought for one moment that he was considering jeopardizing their lifestyle, she would consider him insane. Who would take the risk of squelching the visits to Bali and Rome, limiting the ski trips to Aspen and Vail, sacrificing the summer home in Vermont?

Cameron gripped the pen tightly and added the word *Marilyn* in large block letters to the bottom of the list. He suddenly felt tired. His shoulders ached as if he had been pushing a wheelbarrow full of concrete blocks up a steep hill. He sighed heavily, reached for his bag, and pulled out a bottle of Johnnie Walker.

Now for the cons. He tipped the bottle to his lips and waited for the taste of the whiskey to settle on his tongue. He gripped the pen and began writing, creating a column opposite his first.

Lose my individuality.
Give in to groupthink.
Become one of "them."

He took another long draw on the bottle and frowned. Then he wrote down the line that cut deeply into his soul.

Hurt the people at the end of the line.

What to do? Questions. So many questions. The more he analyzed the issue, the more confused he became. This trip, this time, this exercise was getting him absolutely nowhere. Gripping the pen as if it were his only lifeline, he flipped the paper over and inscribed the word *questions* in large block letters. Then he began writing like a man on a mission, with each inquiry leading to the next in a series of relentless waves.

> *What happens when you surrender your freedom?*
>
> *Can you be truly happy when you silence your own conscience?*
>
> *How much money is enough?*
>
> *Who is responsible for the happiness of the family?*
>
> *Which comes first: Obligations to others or living up to beliefs?*

Cameron stood up and began pacing toward the front of the boat. Beliefs? What beliefs? Did he even have any beliefs? If his conscience were going to interfere with his life, why did it have to pick this very moment?

He walked back to his seat, tightened his grip on the pen, and wrote one last question.

> *Why did I stop going to church?*

He stood, folding the paper, noting the sudden flapping of the flag on the back of the boat. He watched as the wind intensified, whipping up whitecaps and lifting the waves higher.

And then, in the next instant, his list was ripped from his grip and sent airborne.

Cameron watched as a gust of wind carried it high above the boat, sent it careening past a flying tern, and pushed it into the upper levels of the atmosphere. He cupped his hands around his eyes and watched until it became nothing more than a tiny dot that was finally extinguished from his view.

Three

Bob Maggiano flew down Bayside as if his feet had wings. He loved running, loved the feeling of dominating the street, loved knowing he could leave everyone else standing still if he so desired. Bob hated the idea of being second. He despised losers. Effort, determination, and willpower. That's what made the man.

Bob rounded the corner and ran past the stately yellow house he had called home throughout his childhood years. He remembered his father lining all the kids up, checking the creases in their pants, their posture, their fingernails. He hated it when his father called him out. Judged him for some imperfection. Found him to be unworthy of the honor of being part of the Maggiano family.

Cutting to the channel side, Bob sprinted down the path along the water. A line of dinghies bobbed lightly, waiting to be navigated to the yachts moored in the bay. Bob was tempted to sit down on the bench for a moment, catch his breath, and take in the fingers of early morning light spreading a golden wash across the horizon. He checked his watch. It was 6:48 A.M. If he maintained his pace, he could make the mile in under five minutes. He kept running.

Halfway to Oyster Bay, he spotted it. A lone piece of paper, tucked into a clump of beach grass. Bob pursed his lips in disgust. A rush of adrenalin propelled him forward with a new burst of speed. Bob hated litter. There was no need for it. Trash cans were strategically located along the trail. What was the point of randomly throwing garbage wherever and whenever you pleased? People were lazy. What did they think? That the whole outdoors was their personal dump? You might expect something like that on the east side, across the bay, a couple of miles inland. But here?

Imperfection. He had little tolerance for the small things that remained unaddressed. His first wife, Alyssa, just didn't get it. He had picked a long strand of hair off her wedding dress at the altar. That should have been his first clue. When she left the mud on her hiking boots while they were honeymooning in Hawaii, he could almost feel his left eye twitch. But it was the wine glasses rimmed with her rose-blush lipstick that had finished him off.

Bob reached the dock and checked his time. Not bad. Not bad at all. That last spurt of adrenaline had helped. He finished his run at only twenty seconds above his personal record of four minutes and thirty-eight seconds. His goal was to break the four-minute mile. A few more weeks of training and he'd be there.

He slowed to his cooldown pace then to a brisk walk, taking the trail behind the gray stone building of Bay Life Church. He'd tied the knot with his second wife overlooking the harbor here. A handful of close friends had gathered in the outdoor chapel, hoping this one would last. How could it have lasted when MaryAnne started heading to services every Sunday? How could the relationship withstand the pressure of a wife-turned-churchgoer?

He had tried to explain. But what was the point? Once the church got its tentacles around MaryAnne, their relationship was doomed. He'd hated church as a kid. It was all about judgment. You were judged for not sitting up straight. Judged for not wanting to sing. Judged for speaking up in Sunday School. Entire sermons delivered the bad news on judgment. Those Sundays were the worst.

Bob checked his watch. He had a meeting at 8:15 sharp. Time to head home, grab a quick shower, and fire up the computer for his online appointment. Picking up his pace, he cut through the church parking lot and headed across the green.

Judgment Day. The preacher had made it sound like something even Arnold Schwarzenegger couldn't handle. The angels checking the record—examining, analyzing, just waiting to find one mark, one scratch, one slight, one sin, one offense to knock you out of the park for all eternity. And then came the hellfire. Hotter than hot. Blazing, searing, scorching. Always burning but never destroying. Your flesh in flames but never being consumed. Your body blackened but not deadened. Your life over but never ending.

Bob felt the old familiar wave of panic begin to creep upward from his chest. He stuffed it down. He ran faster. He summoned anger. He hated church. Despised religion and faith. It was all garbage. If MaryAnne had never stepped foot in the Bay Life Church after the wedding, they would still be married. She had been a perfect match for him. She lined up the shoes in the closet like they were on military command. She placed her fork at a perfect angle on the plate. She made him proud. Until church.

Something had changed in MaryAnne. She began to find excuses to leave the house. Prayer meetings. Fellowship dinners. Christmas programs. She couldn't understand his anger. She just kept pressuring him. If only he would go to church, things would get better. If only they could talk with the pastor. If only he would go to prayer meeting.

What was the point? Religion was just a tranquilizer for people too weak to make life work on their own terms. He hated to see MaryAnne leave. But it was her choice.

Life was better without her. It gave him more time to do what he needed to do. Go where he needed to go.

The sun landed on a patch of beach grass, illuminating the tufts like sparkling shafts of wheat. Bob frowned. Beach grass. Even beach grass seemed to make him angry. And then he remembered. The careless toss of a hand. The crumpled white paper along the trail. The litter marking his neighborhood like something you'd see on the east side. If he hurried, he would have just enough time to take care of the problem.

Bob turned and began jogging back toward Oyster Bay. The sun was higher now, and beads of sweat popped out on his forehead like water droplets on a glass. The dock at Oyster Bay buzzed with traffic. Early morning fishermen loaded their small boats with poles, bait, and buckets. Silver-haired gentlemen maneuvered their dinghies toward the waiting vessels. A small boy gripped his mother's hand and marched the length of the rough-hewn boards.

Bob rounded the corner and headed for the small park lined with beach grass. If he remembered correctly, the paper had been wedged in the clump of sea oats on the northwest corner of the green adjacent to the running trail. Perhaps someone had already retrieved it. In that case, he would cut through the park and take the shortcut home.

Trash. He hated the stuff. Fortunately, this neck of the woods was not populated by those who didn't care about the neighborhood. It was rare to find even a lone candy wrapper discarded by the wayside. People like him just didn't do that kind of thing.

Slowing his pace, Bob approached the park. It wasn't hard to spot the paper. Still wedged in the beach grass, it glowed white, illuminated by a ray of the sun. Bob stooped and pulled the paper from the reeds. It was folded in a square, the outside smeared as if it had gone through a rainstorm.

Bob stuffed the thing in his back pocket, then checked his watch. There was no time to look around for a trash can. He needed to take the shortcut home and prepare for his day. A brisk shower and a few moments to collect his thoughts ought to do it.

Bob flew past aspens and oaks in no time flat. He slowed to a walk at the gate to his town house and then did a few cooldown exercises in his driveway. He buzzed open the front door and threw his clothes in the waiting hamper before jumping into the shower. After showering, he combed his hair and reviewed his notes. By 8:12 A.M., he was connected and waiting.

A face popped up on his screen. "Weston?" Bob asked. "Weston Reese? So good to meet you."

Four

Cameron Stanton lay wide awake beside his sleeping wife in the king-size bed on the third floor of 212 Blue Anchor Lane. A light breeze blew in through the open window. A boat horn sounded in the distance. Marilyn stirred briefly, then turned on her side and resumed the deep breathing that Cameron could only covet.

It was silly to worry about a piece of paper flying around the Atlantic on the edges of a storm. It was probably totally dissolved on the ocean floor by now. If it had made it to land, there was no chance the thing was intact. It was probably pulp, seeping into the earth. And if it had stayed intact, there was no chance the letters were even readable. And if they were even a tiny bit legible, there was no chance anybody would just happen by and pick it up. And if somebody did pick it up, there was no chance they would catch the context. And if they did catch the context, there was no chance they would make the connection with Weston Reese.

Cameron sat up and swiveled to the side of the bed. He had to stop this insane loop. How many times could he go from one irrational thought to another in the same night? This was ridiculous. Was he on the verge of losing his mind?

He tapped the flashlight icon on his cell phone and headed for the stairs. What had he written on that paper anyhow? The whole thing was so ironic. He had been in the middle of the ocean. Trying to get away from people and land and interruptions. Trying to steer clear of everybody's opinion. And then he lost control of the object that represented all of it.

He took the last two stairs in one long step and turned toward the country kitchen, its large farm table silhouetted in the moonlight. Pulling out a chair, he deliberated. Should he try to reconstruct the list? Would that stop the endless flow of questions once and for all? Or would it just stir up his mind further, make sleep even more elusive? Hadn't he read something once? Wasn't there some value in getting everything down on paper? Maybe if he made a list his mind would finally give the whole thing a rest.

He picked up the remote to the dining room light and inched the dial up a notch. *Not too bright. No need to wake myself up even more. Let's just get it done. Side one: pros and cons of joining the business merger.*

Drawing a line down the middle of a blank sheet of paper for the second time that week, Cameron forced himself to think through the late-night fog enveloping his brain. The pros came easily, flowing from the pencil without much thought—money, status, family.

When it came to the cons, Cameron found himself at a loss. He slid his arms forward on the dining room table and cupped his chin in his hands. His head ached. His muscles throbbed. *Why would I even consider opting out of the merger?*

Leaving the cons column blank, he turned the paper over and began jotting down the questions that continued hammering his mind. *What do I have to lose? What is wrong with joining forces? Doesn't strength lie in numbers? Why is this thing bothering me so much?*

He stood up and made his way to the arched window overlooking the bay. The dinghies rocked in dark outlines along the shore. The moon cast a beam of light across the waves. Indigo clouds scurried across the dark sky.

Because I have a conscience, that's why. He turned, grasped the pencil with determination, flipped the paper back over, and began filling in the left column with bold strokes.

CONS:
My decisions will no longer be my own.
I will sacrifice integrity for personal gain.

Loss of integrity for personal gain. That was it. That was the crux of the whole matter. Integrity. He had been raised to care about things like that. Raised with a conscience. Raised to believe in God. Raised to pray. Maybe it was time to go back to his roots.

For the first time in decades, Cameron Stanton bowed his head. *I need help, God. I can't let my whole business go crashing down at this stage of the game. We're in deep. Marilyn would never consider cutting back. Jay is on the edge of something good. We're comfortable here. We have a good life. Please, God.*

He took in a deep breath, let it out slowly, and scraped his chair across the flagstone floor. Despite the conflict within him, he felt a hint of peace tease the edges of his mind. The thought of sleep dangled within the realm of possibility. He had turned things over to God. It was time for bed.

On the third floor, he approached his room with light steps, turned the door handle slowly, and prepared to enter the shadowy interior. Just as he was about to step over the threshold, a beam of light shone from behind.

"Dad?"

For a moment, Cameron felt his heart stop. Jay had awakened him only once in the past decade. Although it had been two years now, Cameron remembered that night like it was yesterday. The rain dripping from the eaves. Jay's light tap on the door of the master bedroom. The cell phone still in his hand. The accident that had claimed the life of the girlfriend he had loved since kindergarten. Marilyn sitting up in bed, dazed. The heavy weight of it all. The burden of being a father and having nothing to say. The crushing realization that you had never offered your son anything more valuable than money.

Now Jay stood in his plaid pajama shorts, his thick, dark curls slightly mussed, a look of fear clouding his features.

In his right hand, he trained a small flashlight along the mahogany floor. In his left, he held a thin white envelope.

"Dad? Can we go downstairs? I need to talk."

Five

Bob Maggiano couldn't believe his good luck. Time to check his horoscope. The stars must be aligned just right. In his wildest imagination he never would have dreamed that Weston Reese would even consider him as a business partner.

Bob pulled back the navy-blue covers, jumped out of bed, smoothed the sheets, tucked in the ends with perfect hospital corners, and slipped into the jogging clothes he had set out the night before.

He was on his way now. Making his way up. Climbing the gilded staircase. Passing the crowd. He could almost smell the money.

But beneath it all something else stirred, threatening to dampen the elation. He wanted to share the news. Call a family member or a friend and go over all the details. Have a few drinks. Laugh. Feel the warm pat on the back. Celebrate with someone.

But who was there to call? Bob chugged a bottle of water and headed down the hall. Larry would have been the obvious choice a year ago. He'd always had a spotty relationship with his older brother, but at least they used to talk. All it took was one phone call to end things. Larry just didn't want to listen when Bob brought up the weight problem. His brother needed to face the music. The pounds were not going to disappear by themselves. He needed discipline in his life. Exercise. Diet.

Bob bent down and tied his Swiss-engineered running shoes. A folded piece of paper fell from his back pocket, landing on the tile floor beside him. He frowned, then remembered collecting the litter during yesterday's run. He unfolded it slowly. A faded line ran down the middle, a semblance of dissolved letters running down the sides. Absentmindedly he turned the paper over. The back side of the paper was clean and readable.

A string of boxy green letters appeared on top, spelling out the word *questions*. Despite himself, Bob backed against the wall and began to read.

What happens when you surrender your freedom?

What kind of a question was that? What freedom? Life was about discipline. Guys like Larry needed to surrender their freedom. They needed some structure in their lives.

> *Can you be truly happy when you silence your own conscience?*

Who wrote this? Some kind of religious freak like MaryAnne and the Bay Life Church crowd?

> *How much money is enough?*

Bob straightened up and began pacing around the house. What kind of a dumb question was that? More money equaled more opportunities. Pretty basic equation.

> *Who is responsible for the happiness of the family?*

This guy was all over the map. What did the family have to do with money, freedom, and your conscience?

> *Which comes first: Obligations to others or living up to beliefs?*

Bob felt his blood pressure rising. Religious freaks were taking over the planet. Why ask such ridiculous questions? People who wrote stuff like this were just trying to prove their intelligence. He'd met them all before. They walked around with their judgmental noses stuck in the air, acting like theologians.

Bob grabbed a pen from the kitchen counter and added another question to the bottom of the list.

> *Why would anyone be dumb enough to believe in God?*

He stuffed the paper in his back pocket, swung open the door, and began stretching his quads. A string of bikers rolled out of the development, their helmets reflecting the rays of the early morning sun. Bob did ten hip rotations on each side, twenty lunges with side bends, a dozen lateral squats, ten calf stretches. Then he headed for the road.

A light breeze blew in from the bay, rustling the beach grass along the trail. A red- shouldered hawk wheeled over-head, whistling plaintively. Bob maintained a steady pace, overtaking slower runners without a nod. Passing the Bay Life Church, he noted a few cars pulling into the parking lot. Religious freaks! Praying at this time of the morning?

Bob rounded the bend in record time. The full sweep of Oyster Bay came into view. Only a few early morning fishermen appeared on the dock, their buckets and poles forming shadows on the rough wooden pier. The dinghies bobbed in gentle rhythm beside the dock.

Catching the grandeur of the yachts anchored offshore, Bob allowed himself the luxury of a dream. *One of those could be mine in a year. Play my cards right. Hang with Weston Reese. Follow the rules. Collect the cash.*

His eyes fell on a luxurious Sun Odyssey, commanding the bay in regal splendor. *Give me twelve months of big business. I'll take that one. Bob Maggiano, captain of the high seas.*

With a new burst of energy, he cut a sharp right, heading up the hill toward the park. Passing a gleaming row of beach grass, he was suddenly aware of the weight of the single piece of paper occupying his back pocket. He felt compelled to discard it, rid himself of the trash once and for all. The more he thought about it, the more the words made him uncomfortable. He felt guilty, like he'd been blamed—like he was a teenager again, hiding from Sunday School in the bed of his father's truck in the church parking lot.

Are you kidding me? A piece of paper? Get a grip, Bob. Next trash can, it's gone.

Rounding the bend, he passed a neat row of colonial houses. An older woman wearing a blue apron was sweeping the steps of the white house on the corner. As he passed, she lifted her head and her face brightened as if he were her long-lost son returning from war. Waving furiously, she caroled cheerfully, "Good morning!"

Bob whipped his head toward the street, avoiding her gaze. What was her problem? He didn't even know the woman.

At the park, a young man was pushing a small girl on a swing. An elderly couple sat at a picnic table sipping coffee. Three gray squirrels engaged in a game of catch-me-if-you-can.

Bob slowed his pace and reached for his back pocket. He approached the trash can in its black wire holder. Just as he prepared to toss in the paper, he noted a new addition to the park. Below the overhang in front of the rest rooms, a green frame was attached.

Inside the freshly painted wood, a corkboard prominently sported the phrase *Community News*. A row of tacks lined the bottom of the board.

A slow smile began to spread across Bob's face. Perfect. They wanted community news. He was going to give it to them.

He unfolded the paper, particularly pleased with his addition to the list.

Why would anyone be dumb enough to believe in God?

Pulling a tack from the board, he attached the paper with relish. Then he wheeled around, put his Swiss-engineered sneakers into high gear, and headed home.

Six

Alice Jones was on a roll. In the past few days, she had weeded her garden, done three loads of laundry, baked four loaves of bread, and read an entire commentary on Revelation 14. Humming as she dusted the back of Lance's dining chair, she thought about the beginning of the first angel's message. "Fear God and give glory to Him, for the hour of His judgment has come" (verse 7).

Fear God. Too bad the words had such a different ring in today's world. Most people didn't stop to find out the real meaning. There was no need to be put off. *Fear God* didn't mean to be afraid of Him. That would be a sad state of affairs. Instead, it meant we should respect, honor, obey, worship.

Alice checked her watch. It was 9:00 A.M. In just twenty minutes, Janet would drop off Fleur. She'd better hustle if she wanted to finish her housework. She made her way to the kitchen and began retrieving an arsenal of disinfectants, scrubbers, and polishes from beneath the sink. There was something satisfying about making your house clean, sponging away grime and killing germs. Alice filled the sink with steaming hot water, squeezed in a stream of Mr. Clean, thrust her hands into her yellow plastic gloves, and submerged a white rag in the water. Now she was ready for battle.

Wiping down the counters, she continued to let her thoughts flow. *Give God glory because His judgment has come.* That sounded like an oxymoron. An evident contradiction. Why would you glorify someone for judging you? It had taken her a long time to get to the bottom of that one. She had never liked being judged in school. Science fairs. Fifty-yard dashes. Spelling bees. Poetry contests. A few kids took the prize and everyone else went home disappointed.

Alice paused, dipped the rag in hot water, squeezed the water out, and began scrubbing the stove. *Give God the glory, for the hour of His judgment has come. Jesus the Supreme Judge is in your corner. And He offers His own perfect life to make sure you win. Imagine a science fair judge telling you, "No problem. I got this. Your experiment's a little off, but you can use mine."* Alice snickered at the thought. *Or the judge of a spelling bee. "Incorrect. Let me spell it for you, so you can stay in the competition." Or how about an English teacher reading your poetry submission? "The piece lacks rhythm and appears rather bland, but let me substitute my own poetry for yours."*

That was it! *The poetry of Christ's life for ours. The perfect rhythm, meter, and rhyme. The flawless life, covering, cleansing, purifying our own.*

The words hummed through Alice's mind as she completed her routine. She finished her cleaning quickly, anxious to grab her journal and get it all down. She loved words. She enjoyed the flow of syllables creating life and meaning on the page.

The poetry of Christ's life for ours. The perfect rhythm, meter, and rhyme. The flawless life, covering, cleansing, purifying.

She penned the sentences with a flourish, pleased with herself for putting into words the depth of Christ's selfless act. Closing her journal, she offered a silent prayer of gratitude. She was a woman alone, but her life was in God's hands.

Outside, footsteps sounded on the front porch. Alice swung the door open wide, revealing Fleur straining at the leash, two jaunty red bows contrasting with her white fur. Barking excitedly, the poodle greeted Alice with a series of rapid licks to her outstretched hands.

"Thanks so much for offering to walk her." Janet slipped the leash into the older woman's hands. "I never dreamed working at home would leave me with *less* time rather than more."

"No problem at all. Glad to do it." Alice closed the door behind her and choked up on the leash. "As long as Fleur gets the hang of parading around with an experienced dog-walker, we'll be fine!"

A stray breeze blew in from the bay, lending a salty tinge to the air. Alice headed to the end of Maritime Drive, deliberating. Should she take Fleur down to Oyster Bay and let her prance up and down the dock, delighting the crowd with her antics? Or perhaps Fleur would prefer the park and the enclosed area where she could run with other small dogs.

Alice hesitated. Something deep inside her stirred. She had prayed that morning that God would direct her steps. Walking a dog seemed like such an insignificant thing. But for some reason, she felt the pull of the Spirit. God was taking her on a mission. She could feel it.

With determined steps, Alice cut to the right and began walking down the hill toward the bay. Halfway to the waterfront, she stopped. She had heard about the annual migration of baitfish on the news last night. A crowded dock full of fishing lines was no place for a small dog.

Alice knelt down beside the small white poodle. "What do you think, Fleur? How about we do a little about-face and find you some friends?"

The park dazzled in the early morning sun. A flock of white ibis strolled through the center, scratching for treasure in the sandy soil with their sharp red beaks. Clumps of backlit beach grass swayed in the light breeze. Alice strode past the fence bearing the sign that said Large Dogs and toward the enclosed area behind it reserved for smaller breeds. Swinging open the gate, she let Fleur off the leash. The poodle ran for the far fence, elated with her newfound freedom. A Yorkshire terrier ran in circles beside her, eager to make friends. Alice sat on the bench, rehearsing all the details of Fleur's adventure to share with Janet later.

By eleven o'clock, the poodle had worn herself out. Alice clipped the leash to the animal's collar and bent down beside her. "I'm not going to carry you home, Fleur. You've got to make it back to the house now."

Leading the way down the path, Alice headed for the center of the park. Skirting past the restrooms, she was surprised to find a new feature. Below the overhang, a green frame boasted a corkboard filled with community news.

"Well, what do we have here, Fleur?"

The poodle took advantage of the pause, lying down before the board. Alice scanned the papers tacked to the cork. Fall mullet run. Fishing contest. Seaside School fall festival.

At the bottom of the board, a tattered piece of white paper appeared to be out of place. At the top, someone had penned the word *questions* in boxy green letters. Alice cocked her head to the side as she considered the questions.

What happens when you surrender your freedom?

"That's a good one." Alice's heart beat with conviction as she spoke her thoughts into the morning air. "Once you let go of your freedom, you become a pawn. You just start following the crowd."

Can you be truly happy when you silence your own conscience?

Who wrote this? Someone was struggling with a very real issue. Someone needed help. Alice felt her pulse quicken. God had sent her on a mission this morning. She was sure of it. She turned and scanned the park for possibilities. The two moms sitting on a bench while their babies napped in their carriages? The older gentleman sipping a cup of coffee at the picnic table?

How much money is enough?

It was a business issue. Somebody was conflicted. Alice bowed her head. *Lord, be with the writer of this list. Bless the person, whoever it is—man or woman. Give them peace.*

Fleur sighed from her spot on the ground. Alice continued reading.

Who is responsible for the happiness of the family?

So there was a family involved. Someone was trying to make a decision that affected more lives than just their own.

Which comes first: Obligations to others or living up to beliefs?

Bottom line: Somebody was feeling pulled between family and money.

Why would anyone be dumb enough to believe in God?

Alice moved closer to the board. This was clearly not the same person. The writing was slanted to the left and the letters were written in black ink. As offensive as the question seemed, it, too, represented the struggles of a human heart. Alice's heart pounded. Pulling her phone from the bag around her neck, she snapped a picture of the scarred sheet.

Urging Fleur to rise, she charted the course toward Maritime Drive. Time was a'wasting. She had work to do. Alice the warrior was hatching a plan.

Seven

Cameron Stanton closed the exterior door of the office and began pacing up and down the parking lot. The last thing he had expected to find in the envelope in Jay's outstretched hand was a Bible study. He had thought it would be the letter from Harvard or Yale inviting Jay to come for a visit. He had expected to sit down and hear an impassioned appeal from Jay to be prepared for a big college bill. Jay had hinted at the topic before. There was no guarantee of a scholarship. Jay needed to know his father had him covered.

Cameron walked past a row of bright red hibiscus lining the edges of the walk. A Bible study? Jay? Marilyn had insisted they raise their son without the shackles of organized religion. He was a good boy. They had given him morals, values, manners. But religion? Not a chance. Jay didn't know the difference between the Garden of Eden and the Garden of Gethsemane. He wouldn't recognize Moses if he appeared beside a burning bush.

Cameron headed for the Volvo parked at the far end of the lot. When Jay's girlfriend had suddenly lost her life in the auto accident, Cameron's son had withdrawn into himself. There was nothing much any of them could say. Cameron had felt helpless, inadequate—like an ineffective father. Why had he let Marilyn talk him into such a hollow existence?

Jay's question the night before jarred him. "What happens to people when they die, Dad?"

Cameron had motioned to the stairs, trying frantically to gather his thoughts while the two of them padded down to the living room. Heaven or hell. Those were the two options. Christina had been a sweet girl. Encouraging. Kind. He couldn't imagine her experiencing the searing pain of flames while father and son seated themselves on the leather couch, the grandfather clock ticking away the moments of eternity.

"I know we haven't spoken much about religion in this family." It had sounded like an apology, a disclaimer, an excuse, a confession. "Your mother and I didn't want to confuse you or sway you one way or the other."

Cameron started the Volvo, made his way out of the parking lot and onto Birdseye.

"I'm asking, Dad. I really want to know." Jay had looked so intent. Vulnerable and serious at the same time. Cameron cut left and headed toward Northside. He had promised

Marilyn not to spoil Jay with religious notions at a young age, but his son was almost in college, for heaven's sake.

"Our lives go on, Jay," he had finally managed to say. "Christina's soul is with God. She will never face pain again."

He would never forget the look on Jay's face or the bitter twinge to his words. "Really, Dad? She's somewhere floating around in the universe? Her soul is with God? And what about her body? And her mind? Can she hear our conversation? Does she know her parents got divorced because they couldn't take losing a daughter? Does she hear her mother crying every night?"

Cameron had sat on the edge of the couch, staring at his son. No words were coming to his mind. He had enjoyed Sunday School as a child. But he'd been a kid. He'd never asked those kinds of questions. He'd just loved the colorful pictures, the songs lifting the rafters of the church, the steaming casseroles at potluck.

"I went to a Bible study after school, Dad. I'd always hoped there would be an answer. But I just can't buy it. I was wishing there was more."

Jay had cried then, put his arms around his father's neck and sobbed like he was a little boy again, deprived of the only thing that would make his world right. Cameron remembered holding him tightly in the dark, searching his soul for something to say to make his son's pain go away. But there were no words.

Cameron pulled into a spot by the pier, cut the engine, and sat in the car overlooking the bay. He had failed his son.

Failed his wife. Failed himself.

Moored offshore, the Sun Odyssey yacht rose majestically with the waves. What was the point? Cameron shook his head. Boats, cars, a big house. It all led to nothing.

He swung open the car door and walked to the pier. The sun was just beginning to set. A bright path of light cut a swath across the sea. Red and gold rays danced on the waves. A small group gathered on the dock, gazing at the nightly performance with fresh wonder.

Cameron sucked in his breath at the view. He loved this time of evening. The problems of the day disappeared in the cool air; the nightly bedding down of the sun filled his soul with a sense of calm. Each evening, day turned to night. You could count on it. And each morning, the sun came up again without fail.

There has to be a God. Cameron gazed at the waves flowing toward the shore. *The tides come just so far and no farther. The planet provides everything needed for life. And the loveliness of it all. In a godless universe, why the luxury of beauty?*

Life after death? Cameron couldn't answer that one. But why would a celestial being stoop down and create all of this if there weren't something more later?

Cameron stood rooted to the spot, watching until the last glimmer of light faded into blackness. He thought about the sudden stirrings of his soul in the last few days. The pressure from Weston Reese. His own conscience begging for attention. The competing values of supporting his family and living up to his personal convictions. And now this from Jay. It was the last thing he had expected from his son.

But this new revelation changed things. Now it was only Marilyn that stood in the way of courage. Jay needed more than money right now. He needed faith, belief, a foundation to build his life on.

Cameron turned and walked slowly down the dock. The smallest slice of moon offered a pale light in the western sky. Cameron picked up his pace. He would make up for the lack in Jay's life if it was the last thing he did.

Eight

Pastor Vic Morales tidied a few papers on his desk while he waited for Alice Jones to arrive. He worried about his congregation perched beside the bay. When he had arrived in the district four months ago, he had discovered a self-sufficient, mostly aging congregation, perfectly happy to continue with business as usual. Their budget was balanced. Their grounds were neat and tidy. Their fellowship hall was brightly decorated with blue and yellow silk flowers in vases on every table. And nobody in town knew the church existed.

Pastor Vic had first realized the gravity of the problem when he pulled into a sandwich shop just two miles down the road from the church on his first day as a pastor. "Can you point me to the Northside Seventh-day Adventist Church?" he'd asked. The blank looks confused him. Was it possible he had made a wrong turn somewhere?

Eventually he'd spotted the church sign, which was tucked behind a flowering pink bougainvillea bush. The congregation was happy to receive him. They appreciated his sermons. They validated him each time he checked off a name on the shut-ins' visitation list. All was well in Northside. Or was it?

Vic lifted his head just as Alice Jones came bustling into the office looking as if she might burst at any moment. Her fading brown hair was swept into a bun and her gray eyes glinted with energy and purpose. Flouncing into the nearest office chair, she held up her cell phone as if she had won a prize. "Wait until you see this!" she pronounced. "Pastor Morales, we have our marching orders."

Not waiting for a response, Alice launched into the plan she expected the pastor to execute. "Someone posted this list in the park," she explained breathlessly, enlarging the words to the first question on her phone screen. "If you stop and think about it, each one can be explained in light of the three angels' messages."

Pastor Vic leaned forward and read the first question aloud.

What happens when you surrender your freedom?

"Don't you see?" Alice spoke quickly, concerned at the slight furrowing of his brow. "I've been studying the three angels' messages. The verses are all about following your conscience, refusing to surrender your personal freedom.

And look at the other questions. They all fit. The Holy Spirit has been moving on someone's heart."

The pastor studied the screen in Alice's outstretched palm as she enlarged each question and scrolled down. He motioned for her to stop as she approached the final two questions.

Why did I stop going to church?

"Interesting. The questions begin on a theoretical level. Hypothetical almost. But then the writer drills down to something very personal. There's an issue here. A backstory of some kind."

Alice nodded, not sure of the theoretical, hypothetical stuff, but pleased that the pastor was being drawn in despite himself. Finally, she enlarged the screen for the last question.

Why would anyone be dumb enough to believe in God?

The pastor straightened up, taking a breath. "Alice Jones, I'm not sure what to make of this. I find the last question rather offensive."

"But it's not the same writer." Alice felt the old worry creeping into her mind. She pulled her shoulders back, willing herself to become Alice the warrior. "Can't you see the change in handwriting? And they both need God. They both need to understand the three angels' messages. The second half of the first angel's message is all about God the

Creator. We can explain the Genesis story, show some slides about the marvels of nature . . ."

"Slides? What are you building up to, Alice?" Pastor Vic felt his heart rate notching up. He had been concerned about the congregation's invisibility in the community, but his plan had been to gradually introduce the church to the public. Trim down the bougainvillea obscuring the sign. Slip a few flyers under doors. Give out Thanksgiving baskets to those in need.

"We can hold meetings near the park. There's an outdoor amphitheater behind the library. They usually have concerts there, but I'm sure we can make it work. We can go for three consecutive weekends. That should be enough time to cover the three angels' messages."

"I don't know, Alice."

"The writer of these questions is looking for a response, Pastor Morales. Why would someone post a list like this in a public place if they didn't want answers? And who better to reply than us? What better place to find answers than in the Bible? When better to respond than now?"

Alice slipped her phone into the hand-sewn pouch with determination. "Jesus is coming soon, pastor. It's our job to get people ready."

Pastor Vic stood up. Nothing in seminary had prepared him for this moment. The whole thing seemed preposterous. A random note tacked to a board leading to a series on the three angels' messages in a town that had never really heard of Seventh-day Adventists? Where would they even begin? And how could they be guaranteed the mysterious note writers would be in attendance?

"I've been taking free classes in desktop printing at the library," Alice said as she opened her binder and withdrew a colorful poster. "I've taken the liberty to move forward with a few dates, but we can always change them if you think it's necessary. I figured we might start in three weeks. Give people a chance to find their way back to the bulletin board in the park. Give you a little time to prepare."

Pastor Vic took the flyer with trepidation. Large, boxy green letters ran across the top to create the headline "Have questions? Find answers."

Alice Jones clearly meant business. The poster was clear, crisp, direct. She had taken her time with the copy, clearly aiming the words at the unknown individual who had bared his soul to the passing public. Pastor Vic's eyes fell on the bulleted list that Alice had composed beneath the poster's heading.

- Find out what will happen to your personal freedoms in the days ahead.
- Learn why it's important to listen to your conscience.
- Hear why scientists believe in intelligent design.

He continued reading, still dumbfounded at the turn of events placing him front and center in a series of meetings he could barely conceive of creating.

- Opening session October 18.

- Saturday and Sunday nights at 7:00 P.M. during three consecutive weekends.
- Outdoor amphitheater behind the library.

Alice regarded him expectantly, meeting his gaze with a look that dared him to back down. The light from the window framed her face, illuminating a few stray tendrils that had escaped the bun. Outside, the cars of the early arrivers could be heard pulling into the parking lot for afternoon prayer meeting.

Pastor Vic Morales took off his glasses. Rubbed his eyes. Bowed his head. Prayed for strength. Faced Alice. Placed the flyer back into her outstretched hands.

"No need to change the dates, Alice. We'll go with the plan as written."

Nine

Eleni Andreas packed her cleaning supplies and slid them into the back seat of the Chevy waiting in the circular drive of 310 Sandhill Court. She hated paying for a ride to get home from work, but there was no other option. Transmission problems did not fix themselves. And money did not grow on trees, as her father always loved to say.

Back at the efficiency apartment, she looked longingly at the sofa bed in the corner of the room. Her back and legs ached. The sides of her feet chafed against the inside of her sneakers. Her head throbbed. But her physical problems paled in comparison to the tumult brewing in her head. Eleni walked to the sink, turned on the tap, filled a plastic cup, and drank the tepid water in one long gulp. What was she going to do?

For starters, she could barely afford the one-room apartment. She had drained her savings to get into the place.

The rent would be due in three weeks. More than half of her income would be gone each month just to occupy this small space. And then there were all the other bills: electricity, food, cell phone, gas. Not to mention the looming car repairs. But what other options did she have?

Eleni sat down on the corner of the mattress and began massaging her temples. When she'd first moved in with Chad, he'd been so charming. Picking up takeout every night on his way home from his job at the car wash. Driving her around in his Mustang with the top down. Showing her off to his friends.

Showing her off to his friends—that should have been her first clue. She wasn't a piece of merchandise. Eleni sighed. Leaving Chad was the right thing to do. The bruises on her arms told the whole story. But how was she possibly going to make it?

Eleni picked up her phone and scrolled through the contacts. Who could she call? There was no mother, no father to pick her up and dust her off. She wouldn't recognize the woman who had given birth to her if she came face-to-face with her at the checkout line in the grocery store. Life had been one bad foster home after another. Eleni lit a cigarette and took a long drag. She held it between her fingers for a few moments then and crushed it out on a saucer. Smoking was a bad habit. She needed to stop. Especially now.

Eleni checked her watch. The sun would be setting in an hour. She needed to get out of this place, catch some rays, breathe some fresh air, get out of her own head. She grabbed a hooded sweatshirt and headed for the door.

On the lawn behind the apartment, Eleni deliberated. She was unfamiliar with this part of town. She knew only one small section of Northside from the home she cleaned each week. It had been a stroke of luck that she'd found the rental in the first place. She had just turned off the vacuum cleaner when she overheard the homeowner talking on her cell phone about a house around the corner leasing an efficiency connected to the garage. "It's not right," Lorraine had complained. "What kind of people are going to be attracted to the neighborhood? The next thing you know, it won't be safe to walk your dog."

Eleni checked her surroundings. Sprawling homes with sweeping lawns graced a winding country lane. A walking trail ran parallel to the road then wound upward into a shaded patch of aspen and birch. Eleni felt her spirits rise. Whatever happened, she was here now, on a bright, cool day, enjoying a side of life she had seen only in the movies.

A light breeze rustled the tall pines as Eleni trekked her way beside the road and up the hill into the woods. She remembered the last time she had ventured a walk, having rushed out the door before Chad arrived home, hoping to avoid another of his mounting bad moods.

Eleni stopped and picked a sprig of goldenrod. She felt safe here, protected by the quiet, salt-tinged air. She had not told Chad she was leaving. Just cleared out her things the next day and left while he was at work.

At the top of the hill, Eleni scoped out the lay of the land. The road forked, with the eastern branch opening into a wide, grassy area. She heard children's voices, the sound of a dog barking, a distant fountain. On an impulse, she headed toward the sounds.

Emerging from the trail, she found herself in a neatly manicured community park. Several women sat at a picnic table, passing out deli sandwiches and wrapped pickles. A young dad pushed a little girl on a swing. "Higher!" she squealed each time his hands met her back. "Higher!"

Eleni felt a twinge of despondency. She wasn't like these people. She would never fit in with the tanned women with their perfect lives. She wished she could start over, be born into a family with a dad who pushed her on swings and a mom who laughed with her friends at picnics.

Gradually, the reality of her present-day problems came back, settling on her shoulders like a heavy wool blanket. Beyond money, beyond survival, she had a deeper situation to address. One that could not wait much longer. One that demanded an answer sooner rather than later.

Eleni began to walk quickly toward the far end of the park. What to do?

Who to talk to? She needed counsel, a friend, a shoulder, a parent, a spouse.

Overhead, a bank of clouds drifted in front of the sun. Breezes swayed the beach grass lining the walk.

If You're there, God, I need help. Eleni touched the cross hanging from her neck. *I can't make this decision on my own. It's too big for me, God. Too much for me to handle.*

She felt a sob forming in her throat and increased her stride, fighting to push back the emotion. Arriving at a green-framed bulletin board, she paused. Inside the freshly painted wood frame, a corkboard contained the phrase *Community News*. Maybe there would be side jobs posted. Something extra she could pick up to make more money.

A few colorful posters announced the happenings in the surrounding area. One poster announced a fall mullet run. Well, she could always buy a pole and hope to catch enough fish to fill her freezer when money ran low. Good one—she had never even caught a minnow.

Eleni turned to the pale blue flyer next. "Fishing contest," it read. Yeah, right. Winning the prize was about as likely as answering the door and finding her mother standing there.

Then there was the Seaside School fall festival. The school might be a possibility. Maybe they needed extra help cleaning at night. Eleni pulled a scrap of paper from her pocket, grabbed the pencil hanging from a string on the cork, and wrote down the name of the school.

Just as she began to move away from the board, she caught sight of a tattered white paper tacked to the bottom. She stopped, drawn to the boxy green letters printed across the top. *Questions.* Her eyes quickly scanned the list as the sky darkened above. When she reached the end, she untangled the pencil wrapped in the string.

Questions? She had a question. A big question. Maybe if she wrote it down the knot in her stomach would loosen.

Trembling, she held the pencil, trying to formulate the words. *What do you do . . .* She paused, no longer able to hold back the tears. *What do you do . . .* She wiped her eyes. Looked to the left. To the right. Behind her. *What do you do when your only option is to end the life growing inside you?*

Ten

Alice Jones brewed a cup of chamomile tea and opened her Bible to Revelation 14. If she hoped to serve as hostess of the Three Angels Seminar in three weeks, she had better be ready. She settled in at the kitchen table, prepared to savor the words of the messages slowly—she wanted to let them steep in her mind like the tea bag steeping in hot water.

She felt sure of the introduction to the messages. Get the gospel out to the whole world. All 193 nations, 100 uncontacted tribes, 6,500 languages, and who knows how many people groups. At this point, all she could do was start in her little corner of the world. If God wanted her to do more, He'd have to show her after they finished up at Northside.

Alice blew lightly on the tea and sipped slowly. She loved

the first half of the first angel's message. According to the Bible, she was living in the judgment hour of God!

Even as Alice swept her kitchen, walked Fleur, met with the pastor, or opened a can of soup, Jesus was intervening for His people in the heavenly courts. It almost gave her goose bumps. Someday her name would come up. And then, in the midst of the devil's accusations, Jesus would speak her name so lovingly and so sweetly that it made her want to faint with gratitude. The times she spoke sharply to Lance, her negative thoughts about the last pastor, her lack of faith—none of it would matter. Jesus' sacrifice would cover the layers of her life like a fresh coat of paint that would never fade.

"Thank You, Jesus." Alice spoke the words aloud, her hands cupped around the warm mug. No matter what happened in her life, she was certain of one thing: Jesus' sacrifice was enough.

Eagerly, Alice moved on to the new topic for the day. The second half of the first angel's message. Grabbing her highlighter from the jar in the middle of the table, she marked the second half of Revelation 14:7.

"Worship Him who made heaven and earth, the sea and springs of water."

The messages just kept getting better and better. Of course she would worship Him. Everything about the heavens, the earth, the sea, and the springs of water fascinated her. From the time she was a little girl, she had been filled with wonder at God's handiwork. Take the grass and the sky, for example. What would it be like if the sky were purple and the grass pink? How would you even relax? God knew what He was doing, all right.

Alice approached the window and gazed at the wisps of cirrus clouds floating like tufts of white hair in the upper atmosphere. Lance had loved studying God's universe.

She remembered the time he set up the telescope in the backyard and showed her Orion's belt and the Big Dipper. She had felt so small against the vastness of the night sky. Standing there and clasping Lance's hand under the stars, she'd shivered as he told her the diameter of the observable universe. Ninety three billion light-years. She couldn't even wrap her head around it. She'd gripped Lance's hand tighter. Breathed a silent prayer. Told God she was glad He was the one in charge.

Alice picked up her Bible again and reread the last part of Revelation 14:7. "The heavens, the earth, the sea and the springs of water" (NIV). The first angel's message sounded familiar. Where had she heard those words before?

She tapped her fingers on the oak table and concentrated. The fourth commandment! That was it. The phrases were almost exact. She began flipping back to Exodus 20, feeling like she had just bought a vowel on *Wheel of Fortune*. The Bible was amazing. The book explained itself if you just took your time with it—if you savored the words and let them steep like chamomile tea in hot, steaming water.

"Remember the Sabbath day, to keep it holy." Alice spoke the words she knew by heart. "Six days you shall labor and do all your work, but the seventh day is the Sabbath of the LORD your God. In it you shall do no work: you, nor your son, nor your daughter, nor your male servant, nor your female servant, nor your cattle, nor your stranger who is within your gates. For in six days the LORD made the heavens and the earth, the sea, and all that is in them, and rested the seventh day. Therefore the LORD blessed the Sabbath day and hallowed it."

Alice reached for the highlighter and marked the words in verse 11: "The heavens and the earth, the sea, and all that is in them."

This was no coincidence! God had linked the first angel's message to the fourth commandment like two beads on a chain. But there was more. A third bead. Alice's mind whirred like the Wheel of Fortune about to land on a trip to Hawaii. *The heavens and the earth, the sea, and all that is in them*, she repeated internally. Genesis 1. God fashioning the world with His own hands at the beginning of time.

Alice felt like dancing in the ray of sunlight streaming from the kitchen window. Genesis 1. God the Creator, finishing His work in six days and resting on the seventh. Exodus 20, the command to honor God by keeping the Sabbath day holy. Revelation 14, the call to worship the Creator on the day set aside at the beginning of time.

There was so much to do and so much to share. Alice raced upstairs and scooped up the flyers resting on her desk. It was time to kick into high gear. Northside was about to be turned upside down.

Breathing a silent prayer, Alice opened the front door and marched down Maritime Drive like a woman leading a battalion. Turning toward the park, she swept past a boy on a bike like he was standing still. Above, the cirrus clouds continued their wispy trek across the blazing sky. A flock of white ibis flew in a coordinated pattern.

This was definitely a good day to be alive, Alice decided. Cutting through the playground, she narrowly escaped being clunked in the head by a swinging toddler. Oblivious, she set her course for the far end of the park, swishing past clumps of beach grass lining the path. Arriving at her destination, she smoothed one of the flyers and reached for the tack in her right pocket.

Scanning the board for a good spot, she settled on an empty space to the right of a light-blue poster. She pushed the pin through the upper right corner of the flyer, and she then stopped, her hand frozen in midair. She stared at the tattered white paper tacked below. A new message had been scrawled to the bottom.

What do you do when your only option is to end the life growing inside you?

Alice gasped, grabbed her phone, and snapped a picture. Life. Creation. The touch of the Divine. She couldn't let a life be snuffed out before a poor child even had a chance to live.

Stabbing another tack into each of the remaining three corners of her flyer, she whirled and headed for the nearest bench. She sat down and tapped Pastor Vic's number on her phone. They had work to do: A flyer to revise. A sermon to rework. A young woman to encourage. A baby to save. The first angel's message was the only hope.

Eleven

Bob Maggiano read the email for the fourth time, praying to a God he didn't believe existed that he had somehow gotten the message wrong. What was he missing? Why was this happening? Bob felt ill, like it was Sunday morning again in the yellow house and his father didn't like his clothes, the length of his nails, the slant of his shoulders. Judged. Weighed in the balances and found wanting. Discarded.

Bob headed for the bathroom, bent over the bowl, and lost his breakfast. He slithered to the floor and lay there, sick and incredulous. He had had such high hopes. Business partner to Weston Reese. Executive salary. Mr. Bob Maggiano, captain of the high seas.

The dream dashed to pieces by a single missive.

The email offered no explanation. There was no attempt

at rationalization. No niceties. No apology. Just a few terse lines delivering the message like a rock dropped on his head.

"We are making a few internal changes in the office. As a result, we will not need your services as a business partner."

What to do now? Should he call Weston? Try to get more information? Bob sat up and wiped the back of his neck with a towel. His body was soaked in sweat. He was a mess.

Bob forced himself to stand up. He grabbed his Swiss-engineered running shoes and laced them so tightly his ankles felt like they were popping out of the flesh. He then headed for the foyer, threw open the front door, and faced the sun in a blinding daze of anger and confusion.

Turning his face toward Bayside, he willed his body into motion. A few early morning joggers dotted the path. He steeled his jaw, pretended the joggers were invisible, stared into the distance, pounded the pavement like a dog off the chain. Rounding the bend, he caught the outline of the yellow house, jerked his head away toward a bank of pin oak trees, sucked in his breath, and picked up his pace.

At Oyster Bay, the Sun Odyssey rocked gracefully in the bay, bathed in the early morning light. Bob felt a stream of bile rising in this throat. The vessel taunted him, laughed with the seagulls at his inadequacy. "You will never arrive, Bob," it seemed to say. "Your father was right. You are nothing more than a kid with a broken fingernail and a bad haircut. You're a second-rate traveler, a poor excuse for a human being."

The dinghies rocked from side to side, their oarlocks clattering, their weathered wood creaking. What did he have to live for? What was the universal point, the grand scheme, the significance of it all? He had been judged from the day he was born. What was his purpose? To slink around in the shadow of those greater, the ones who had arrived?

Just past the bay a chilling thought began to play at the corners of his mind. He could return after midnight. Cut one of the dinghies loose. Row out to the Sun Odyssey. Revel in one night of greatness. Sit in the captain's chair under the light of the moon. Tip a Captain Morgan. Be master of his own fate.

And then . . .

Slip into the dark, inky water. Execute his own exit, in charge and totally in command. There would be no one to tell him he was doing it wrong. A silent scream. A pitch-black ending.

Perfection.

Bob pivoted north, the stream of thoughts flowing like the incoming tide. He'd go into work, act normal. Arrive home at 5:00 P.M. Check the house. Line up his shoes in the closet. Clean the refrigerator. Stop the mail. Empty the garbage. Vacuum the living room. Sweep the porch. Pay the bills. Leave everything in perfect order.

Slowly, his grimace turned to a tight smile. Bob Maggiano, master of his own fate.

He turned onto Maritime Drive, jogged in a perfect staccato rhythm as the sun gradually rose in the sky. Passing the white colonial house on the corner, he again noted the crazy lady nodding and smiling at him as if they were best friends. He slowed down, faced her squarely, gave her a direct stare, then swept past, his thoughts still racing. *Look for me tomorrow morning. Will you miss me, lady?*

At the park, he felt the bile rise in his throat again as he witnessed the laughing families, smiling couples, and giggling children. Did no one get it? There was no point. No purpose. You could never reach the bar. Eventually, the crushing reality bore down. Life was one big contest. And your chances of winning life's lottery were very slim.

A ball rolled toward his feet and he kicked it swiftly, sending it over the heads of two middle-school boys running to retrieve it. *Turn around, boys. Run after your toy. Life is about to get real.*

Bob's heart raced, his thoughts churned. Just a few more yards and he would turn, head home, put in a day at the office. He'd carefully and quietly set everything in order on his desk. Clean out the drawers while the others were at lunch. Spray some furniture polish on a towel. Make everything shine.

Bob dashed past tall, waving stalks of beach grass and pivoted to the left of a picnic table full of elementary-school kids. Ran as if his life depended on it. His gleaming watch beeped. He glanced at his wrist, incredulous. He was about to break his record. The perfect four-minute mile.

He'd leave it on the watch. The ultimate reminder. He wasn't a total failure.

Bob pulled up to the park bulletin board, intending to turn like a swimmer kicking off the wall at the end of lap one. A glossy flyer rippled in the sunlight, a set of boxy green letters unabashedly calling for attention.

HAVE QUESTIONS? FIND ANSWERS.

Bob stopped moving. Threw away his last chance at perfection. The perfect four-minute mile evaporated like steam off his running shoes.

- Find out what will happen to your personal freedoms in the days ahead.
- Learn why it's important to listen to your conscience.
- Hear why scientists believe in intelligent design.

The words sounded eerily familiar. Like topics designed to answer questions he'd heard before. Below the poster, a tattered white paper was still tacked to the bulletin board. Toward the bottom of the paper, his own slanted letters dared the watching universe to respond.

Why would anyone be dumb enough to believe in God?

Why indeed? On an impulse, he snapped a picture of the poster, turned, and headed for the last day of his life.

Twelve

Jay Stanton had never held a Bible in his life. Yet here he was, sequestered in a back corner of Northside Public Library, hunched in a carrel with a small black book in his hand. Thumbing through the pages, he searched for the lay of the land. Titles on top of the page offered only slight clues to the contents. He could recognize names, like Joshua, Ruth, and Samuel. Other words baffled him, like Deuteronomy and Ecclesiastes. Some things made total sense. Like Genesis. The beginning, the first book.

Jay kept thumbing, trying to find something—anything—that would stop his obsessive thoughts about Christina. Where was she now? Could she see him? Did she know he hadn't slept a single night since the wreck?

Past the halfway mark, Jay began recognizing a few names. Matthew, Mark, Luke, and John. In kindergarten he had found a book of nursery rhymes in the school library.

> Matthew, Mark, Luke, and John,
> Bless the bed that I lie on.
> Four corners to my bed,
> Four angels round my head;
> One to watch and one to pray
> And two to bear my soul away.

He had asked the teacher what it meant. "What's a soul? Where are they taking it?"

She had looked at him funnily. Told him it was time for recess.

Jay turned the pages slowly now, starting back at Matthew and scanning the print. Perhaps Matthew, Mark, Luke, or John had something to say about souls. Near the bottom of a page, a word jumped out at him.

"Take My yoke upon you and learn from Me, for I am gentle and lowly in heart, and you will find rest for your souls" (Matthew 11:29).

Rest for your soul? Isn't that what he was looking for? Peace, calm, inner harmony deep in his soul. What would happen to his soul when he died? What had happened to Christina's? Did it explode into the universe on the night of the accident? Or was it floating around somewhere?

Jay frowned, held a chunk of pages between his fingers, and moved to the back of the Bible. The top of each leaf contained two bold words, like the guide words in a dictionary. He moved his eyes down the columns, searching for a pattern. Bingo! The section was some kind of index. You could look for a key word and it gave you a name, like the ones in the earlier sections—Genesis, Ecclesiastes, Malachi. But what was meant by the numbers?

Jay arose from his seat and found a librarian replacing books in the stacks. "Excuse me. Can you tell me how to use this index?"

The young woman paused, regarded him curiously, and took the open Bible from his hand.

"Index?"

Jay felt his face begin to redden. "The numbers. The numbers after the words. What do they mean?"

"Ah. The texts." She gestured toward a table. "I am guessing you don't have too much experience with a Bible."

Jay laughed. "Honestly, this is the first time I've ever held one."

"Not a problem. That's what I'm here for. You'll find a list of the books of the Bible in the beginning."

Jay nodded. *Books of the Bible. So the names are called books. Check.*

"The index in back is called a concordance. When you are interested in a topic, you look for the word. There you will find the book, chapter, and verse."

Concordance. Book. Chapter. Verse. He was going to have to learn a whole new vocabulary.

"Let me show you how to find a passage. Let's say you wanted to look up the word *create*. You would start by finding it in the concordance." She turned a few pages and indicated the column of *c*'s. "Here. Genesis one-one means it is found in the book of Genesis, the first chapter and the first verse. So you would turn to the list I showed you in the front, find the starting page for the book of Genesis, and then find the chapter. Once you find the chapter, you look for the verse. Everything is in numerical order. Make sense?"

"I think I get it. Thanks." Jay bent over the Bible and read Genesis 1:1.

"In the beginning God created the heaven and the earth" (KJV).

The words were solid. Assuring, direct, clear. He liked it. "Thanks. Thanks so much. I can take it from here." Quickly flipping to the back of the book, he looked for the *s*'s. Sliding his finger down the column, he stopped at the word *soul*. He was in luck. The text was in the book of Genesis. He knew exactly where to find it.

At the next table, an elderly woman rustled a newspaper. Jay looked up. The electronic clock on the library wall indicated 9:32. Second period. He was missing algebra class.

Returning his focus to the Bible, he navigated his way past Genesis 1:1 to the passage he'd found in the concordance. Genesis, chapter 2, verse 7. Scanning the verse, he found the word *soul* at the end. Jay gave himself a mental pat on the back. He was definitely getting the hang of things.

"And the Lord God formed man of the dust of the ground, and breathed into his nostrils the breath of life; and man became a living soul" (KJV).

Jay's heart began to pound. It was all making sense. In the beginning God created the world. Then He got down in the dirt, put His hands in the mud, and shaped the first person. But He wasn't done. The clay form needed life. So God breathed. Blew His own breath into the clay. His own God-powered, super-energized, electrifying breath into the clay form. And that did it. Life. A living soul.

Jay pulled a notebook out of his backpack and jotted down his finds. *Genesis 2:27. God's breath into the form of a body = a living soul.*

He traced the words with his finger. Christina's soul wasn't flying around somewhere. A soul wasn't some thin slice of white matter winging around the universe.

Your body. God's breath. A living soul. When Christina was born, she took a breath. And on that dark night, when she breathed her last, her body released the life-giving power of God. She was no longer a living soul.

That much was clear. But if she wasn't a soul, was that the end of her?

Jay felt the sudden need to get to his car. He slid the Bible and notebook into his backpack and stood up. Striding past the librarian's desk, he fought to maintain his composure.

Outside, gray clouds had begun to gather. The tops of the sand pines danced in the breeze. A great blue heron took flight over the marsh. Jay started the Elantra and gazed at the sudden drops sliding down his windshield.

Then he grabbed the steering wheel with two hands, bent his head, and shook the car with great, racking sobs.

Thirteen

*A*lice Jones was worried. She checked her text messages for the fourth time in two minutes. Nothing from Pastor Vic. She stirred her lemon balm tea. Tried to focus on the second angel's message. Checked her text messages again.

The recent question added to the list on the corkboard put a whole new light on things. Pastor Vic had to refer to the sanctity of life. The promise of hope. God's power to create and re-create. She of all people knew what it meant to give birth to a child, tenderly rock her, and place her in the arms of an agency. She of all people knew what it meant to be young, afraid, and alone. To start your life over with a hole in your heart, waiting for Someone bigger to fill it with meaning. But you didn't destroy the image of God growing within you to avoid the pain of giving her away, even if it was the hardest thing ever asked of you.

Alice read the last line of the revised flyer one more time: "Discover the spark of the divine in every life."

Was it enough? Would the young woman catch the drift that she carried something precious, something holy? Would the Holy Spirit impress her to read the bulletin board one more time, put a pause on her plans, come to the meetings?

Alice checked her messages again. Time was running out. She needed to post the flyer. Why wouldn't Pastor Vic answer? Was he afraid to broach the topic?

Stop it! Alice lifted her head. She was Alice the warrior, not Alice the worrier.

Time to give it to God and study the second angel's message.

Alice moved the box of assorted teas to the side of the table and opened her Bible to Revelation 14, verse 8. She loved the way the words flowed in the New King James Version.

"And another angel followed, saying, 'Babylon is fallen, is fallen, that great city, because she has made all nations drink of the wine of the wrath of her fornication.' "

Filled with symbols, this one is. Alice was glad she and Lance had taken Bible studies in the mail when they first met. She knew all about the Babylon of Old Testament times. That would probably be a good place to start. Let the Old Testament guide your understanding of the New Testament.

Leafing her way back to Daniel 2, Alice paused and read the story of Nebuchadnezzar in the first twelve verses. She shook her head at the haughty Babylonian king who threatened to kill the guys who couldn't tell him what he'd dreamed. Imagine demanding that somebody tell you what you dreamed, then shouting, "Off with your heads if you don't figure it out by morning!"

People didn't mess around in Babylon, that was for sure. Alice picked up the teapot decorated with blue flowers, added more water to her cup and dunked the tea bag up and down a few times. Then she checked her text messages. Nothing.

Focus, Alice. Focus. She turned back to the Bible on her lap and continued reading, navigating through the remainder of the chapter. Praise God for making everything so clear. Through the prophet Daniel, He revealed the dream and its interpretation to Nebuchadnezzar.

Alice remembered seeing a picture of Nebuchadnezzar's dream at an evangelistic meeting. The king had dreamed about a giant statue made of different metals. Alice imagined the multicolored man looming on the screen. His head glowed in glittering gold. His chest and arms sparkled in silver. His belly and thighs beamed in bronze. His legs boasted the strength of heavy iron. And the feet—the feet were the most interesting part. Part iron, part clay. Two very different mediums. Soft and hard. Unable to mix together.

And then came the stone, which crashed the whole thing to the ground.

A faint bell sounded on Alice's phone. Startled, she grabbed the instrument. It was about time. Pastor Vic must be back to the land of the living.

"Hey, Alice. Your friendly next-door neighbor with a

last-minute request. Are you able to walk Fleur a bit later?"

Alice sighed. Why not? Apparently, she wouldn't be getting together with Pastor Vic anytime soon.

Turning back to Daniel, Alice studied the interpretation of the dream. Centuries ago, God had foretold the history of the world right up to the end of time. The whole thing was incredible!

Alice marked Daniel 2:31–34 with a yellow highlighter. The metals represented kingdoms. Babylon. Media-Persia. Greece. Rome. And the feet? After Rome, there would never be a world kingdom again until the coming of Jesus—the Rock cut without hands.

But then came the mind-boggling part. Alice shifted in her seat. Nebuchadnezzar actually stood there, pretending to take it all in. Then what did he do? He built a statue entirely out of gold and commanded that everyone bow down and worship it.

How could he do such a thing? How could he try to one-up the God who gave and interpreted dreams? How could he attempt to take God's message and make it his own? And then command people to act on his distorted version of the truth? It was hard to imagine such self-centeredness.

And what about symbolic Babylon? How did it connect with historical Babylon and point ahead to the final events to take place on planet Earth? Alice turned her attention back to Revelation 14:8.

"Babylon is fallen, is fallen, that great city, because she has made all nations drink of the wine of the wrath of her fornication."

Suddenly everything began to fall into place. Historical Babylon tumbled to the ground. And symbolic Babylon was waiting in the wings to repeat the narrative. In ancient times, the king took a tiny piece of God's prophecy and tried to rework the coming events, making himself the hero. Nebuchadnezzar mixed truth with error. But he couldn't change history. His kingdom went down. And all the people who believed the lie went down with it.

Alice cleared her things from the table and turned on the tap to rinse the cup and saucer. Babylon falling. In the days ahead, things were going to heat up. Like Nebuchadnezzar, a world leader would rise up. And like the ancient king, he would form dangerous alliances, distort God's word, and ratchet up the demands.

Compliance. Conformity. Crowd mentality. Alice shuddered. She had to be strong. Hold on to Jesus. Keep all ten of the commandments.

Alice dried her hands on a towel. Turning to her journal, she added some notes and reviewed the first and second angels' messages.

Give glory to God for the judgment. His perfect sacrifice is enough.

Worship the Creator. Honor Him on the seventh day.

Babylon will fall. Keep a sharp eye. Don't be deceived by truth mixed with error.

Oh, Jesus, make me ready. Alice bowed her head. *Let me be with my Lance again. Let me see Your beautiful face. Keep me faithful.*

A knock sounded from the front of the house. Alice lifted her head and hastily ended her prayer. She looked around for the treats she'd stashed for Fleur. Grabbing a light sweater from the hook, she headed for the foyer and swung open the door.

"Ready to roll?" Pastor Vic beamed. "If we are going to revise our script, we'd better put our heads together. The lives of three mysterious writers are on the line. And now there's a baby on the way. Let's get moving, Alice. October 18 is just around the corner."

Fourteen

Bob Maggiano sat up in bed, ashamed to face the light of another day. He was a failure. A total, abject failure. He couldn't even manage to leave the planet on his own terms.

The night had been perfect. Cloudless. Black. Barely a moon. The dinghies groaned in the dark, tethered and waiting. The pier was ghostlike. Deserted.

He jumped off the dock, landed in the first of the small boats, which was ironically called *Deliverance*. Slicing the oars through the inky waters, he'd felt the kiss of perfection for the first time in his life. Nobody was there to judge his motives, tell him he was doing it all wrong. He inhaled the cool breeze like a parched traveler tasting water for the first time in days. He pulled and pushed the oars with an energy born of a clear mission. He could do this. Everything was right.

Just ten yards from the Sun Odyssey, he spotted trouble. A dark figure appeared on the yacht, pacing up and down the deck. What was somebody doing on the boat in the middle of the night?

He pushed on the oars, back-paddled, turned the dinghy toward shore under cover of darkness. Was the universe against him? He grabbed the bottle of Captain Morgan and tipped it to his lips, draining half of the thing in fewer than sixty seconds. He lost his nerve. Abandoned the mission. Returned to the dock. Tied up the dinghy like nothing had ever happened. Jogged back to the townhouse. Flopped on the bed and stared at the ceiling. Counted every minute until the sun rose again. A total, complete failure.

Bob slipped out of bed, straightened the covers, and tucked in the sheets with perfect hospital corners. Three weeks had passed since the failed endeavor that played over and over in his head. Twenty-one agonizing, tauntingly similar days. Jog around Bayside. Take a shower. Go to work. Return home.

And today would be the same.

Scrolling through his cell phone, he absentmindedly clicked on the Gallery icon. A photo popped up. A glossy poster with boxy green letters announced a series of meetings at the amphitheater. He checked the date. October 18. Tonight.

Maybe there was a purpose to his life after all. He'd be there. In the back row with the hecklers. Letting these religious fanatics know they didn't belong in Northside. Bob grabbed his toothbrush. Went at his teeth with a vengeance. Kicked off his day with a new purpose.

* * * * *

"Be sure to ask everyone to sign in," Alice Jones reminded Pastor Vic for the hundredth time. "I need to check the handwriting. Compare it to the questioners. Find out if they're here. It'll help to have everything on separate cards so I can examine each one closely."

Victor Morales nodded, attempting a weak smile. The woman was dedicated. He'd give her that. She was committed, prepared, honest. A true servant of the Lord. A bit intense at times, but wasn't that the price of being a details person?

The amphitheater caught the sun's last rays, the concentric tiers of seats warmed and waiting for the guests. Pastor Vic imagined himself pacing across the flat stage, preaching upward to the audience dotting the stone benches around the oval. Was this really happening? Would anyone actually show up in the next hour?

At exactly 7:00 P.M., the first visitor arrived. Alice smoothed the collar of her blazer, selected one of the shiny new pens, and handed a sign-in card to Philip Dunham, first elder of the Northside Seventh-day Adventist Church. He squinted at the empty ring of seats. "Not exactly a bestseller, eh, Alice?"

Ignoring him, she shifted and faced the park. In the distance, a small group approached. Three women she'd seen lunching at the picnic tables were making their way toward the area. "Look," she whispered, elbowing Pastor Vic. "Maybe these are our questioners."

By 7:08 P.M., fifteen people were perched around the ring, listening intently as Pastor Vic opened his Bible. Alice examined the cards and scrutinized the handwriting. Too loopy. Too straight. Too slanted. Not enough slant. She gazed at the faces of the attendees who were drinking in the message from the Bible. God was blessing. But she couldn't help but feel just a little disappointed. Unless they had disguised their handwriting, none of the three questioners were present.

* * * * *

Bob Maggiano kicked himself. Why did he have to work late tonight of all nights? If he hurried, he could make it to part of the meeting. Give these nuts a dose of their own medicine, put them under the spotlight of embarrassment and discomfort they loved to shine on everyone else.

Lacing up his Swiss-engineered running shoes, Bob felt a rush of adrenaline powering him with an energy he hadn't known since the night on the bay. Outside, a cool, salty breeze brought him back to that evening. The wind blowing against his cheek, the velvetlike darkness. He'd had resolve, a sense of purpose, a mission.

He executed his warm-ups. Hamstring stretches. Squat thrust. Side bend. Lunging hip flexor. Then he hit the pavement. He flew past the cluster of townhomes on Eagles

Drive. Swept out onto Birdseye. Ran down Bayside. Cut east.

Bob ran harder, closing the gap between the townhomes and Northside Park. They wanted to judge him? Let them judge. Verdict? Christian-hater. Atheist. Guilty as charged. His heart raced in his chest. He anticipated the members of the crowd turning, craning their heads in shock as he interrupted the speaker and called out, "Not true!" "I object, Your Honor." "No God. No judgment. No burning hellfire!"

Charging past the yellow house, he cried into the rushing air, "You're not the judge of me!" He flew around the corner. Bob Maggiano. Captain of the high seas. Master of his own fate.

Just another mile. A slight turn down Maritime Drive. Turning left, he pounded past the white colonial on the corner. *Where are you tonight, crazy lady? I thought we were friends.*

Glowing carriage lights created pools of gold on the deserted road. A nighthawk sounded his sharp call. A sweet pine scent tinged the air with a hint of holiday.

On the fringes of the park, Bob slowed his pace. The swings swayed in the semidarkness. Picnic tables rested quiet, empty. The cork bulletin board sent a boxy shadow along the path.

He paused, turned toward the amphitheater. Sucked in his breath. Listened. A stream of sound projected into the night air. Cocking his head, Bob began to pick up a few phrases. "We are living in . . ." "Has come . . ." "God's timetable . . ."

Bob crept closer. He could see the ring of seats now, the small, scattered group leaning forward, the speaker pacing on the stage. "God's judgment hour . . ."

The judgment! Bob could feel his pulse quicken. Out of instinct he pivoted, jogged back to the park, and sat down on a picnic bench. He didn't need to subject himself to that. Was judgment the only thing Christians wanted to talk about? God looking down from heaven and finding you wanting? Imperfection? Being caught at the end with no excuse?

He reached down and tightened a shoelace. Stood up. Stretched his hamstrings. Headed out of the park. He ran down Maritime Drive, a lone figure briefly illuminated by the golden carriage lights before disappearing into the blackness. Just past the white colonial, he slowed his pace.

The nighthawk screeched above. A slice of moon slipped from behind a bank of clouds. A salt-laden breeze rustled tall shafts of beach grass. Bob pulled himself up short. What was he doing? Epic failure number two. First the bay, now the amphitheater. He had planned this night. Designed the whole thing. And he was aborting the mission?

With fresh resolve he whirled, cut a swath through the woods beside the trail. He needed this night. Needed to confront the Christian hypocrites. Needed to face his demons. The judgment. His father's left eyebrow rising in disapproval. Weston Reese sending the curt email that broke his hope. A dark figure pacing the deck of a boat he could never own.

Bob was out of breath by the time he reentered the park.

He walked past the shadowy swings. Slowly circled the picnic tables. Moved closer to the amphitheater.

Arriving at the stone seats, he hesitated. He had planned on sitting in the back.

But where was the back in an oval of graded rows?

The speaker paced on the center stage. A dark, short man. Intense. Arms outstretched, palms up.

Bob followed the hill down, balanced himself on the steep grade by walking sideways. He stopped at the front row, an arm's length from the stage. He lifted his right foot over the low wall, then his left and dropped his body onto the bench.

The speaker wheeled on the stage. Headed in his direction.

Is this the time? Concentrate, Bob. For once in your life, get the timing right. Listen to the words. Throw the perfect punch. Make a commotion.

The pastor was almost even with him now. He rocked on the balls of his feet. Met Bob's eyes with a kind yet intense gaze. Spoke in a warm, appealing voice unlike any preacher Bob had ever heard.

Bob leaned forward. Focused.

"Imagine the scene. You are facing the judgment bar of God."

The hair on the back of Bob's neck began to stand up. He grabbed the corner of the wall. Prepared to exit. But something in the night air kept him in his seat.

"The record is read. Every slight in your life is exposed to the watching universe." Bob squirmed. Coughed. *This is your moment, Bob. Now. Get ready to yell.*

The pastor continued to meet his gaze. "The devil laughs. He has done his work. His temptations have trapped and ensnared you."

Bob rose to his feet. *Now, Bob. Now.* A trickle of cold sweat ran down his back. His heart pumped with fear and anticipation.

"And then Jesus enters the scene. Lifting His wounded hands before the Father and the holy angels, He calls your name. 'He's mine.' "

The pastor came closer to the edge of the stage. Stooped forward. Met Bob at eye level.

" 'I know him by name,' Jesus says. 'My love extends beyond his problems. I forgive every slight, forget every imperfection. I remember his sin no more. He shall walk with Me in white. Through My blood, he is worthy.' "

Worthy? Bob Maggiano, worthy?

Bob held on to the words. Rolled them around in his head. Dared to believe them. His imperfections did not matter. Christ was on his side. God did not want to judge him. He wanted to save him!

He opened his mouth. Gathered courage. *Now, Bob. Now.* He let forth a shout. Watched as seventeen heads turned his direction. Stood stunned against the night sky, incredulous at the phrases streaming from his own lips.

"Hallelujah! It's not about me! Praise God for the judgment!"

Fifteen

Eleni Andreas swept her dark mane into a ponytail, threw on a bulky gray sweatshirt, and headed into the night. She knew the way to the park by heart now: the walking trail parallel to the road, the clump of trees clustered on the side of the hill, the dirt road branching and the fork leading to the wide grassy area, the opening revealing the swings. She had hiked the trail every night since discovering the path three weeks ago.

She ventured out into the blackness of midnight, the light from her cell phone illuminating the way. Surrounded by the night calls of owls, the low moan of the foghorn, the wheeling and dipping of the wind, she walked. Thinking, gripping the crucifix around her neck, and praying.

She was early tonight. Seven o'clock. She had thinking to do. A decision to make. One last night of imploring the skies above for an answer. One way or the other, she had promised herself the agony would be over by tomorrow.

Eleni retrieved a cigarette and lighter from her jeans pocket, snapped a flame in the darkness, shattered the silent woods with a sharp *click*. She inhaled once, then threw the cigarette to the dirt, stomped it to the ground with her faux leather boot.

The decision was too big. How could she make it alone? She checked her cell phone. In the past three weeks she'd heard nothing from Chad. She slid her fingers across the screen. Hesitated. If Chad knew, would he take her back? Help support them? Pick up extra shifts at the car wash?

She remembered the nights he'd walked into the apartment calling her name, the smell of fried chicken filling the room as he plopped the box on the table while the TV played in the background. It was their shared joke— Kentucky Fried by candlelight.

She stared at the cell phone. Chad was the closest thing to home she had ever known. The only one who had stood by her. Rubbed her back after a hard day scrubbing floors.

Something like hope hovered around the corners of her mind. They could do this.

Together. They could make it work.

She tapped her finger on Chad's number. Waited. One ring. Two. Three. And then his voice, real, live, deliberately robotic: "This is Chad Johnson. I'm sorry. I don't recognize the call-back name, Eleni Andreas. Please hang up and bother someone else. My girlfriend and I are not interested."

He cut off the call then, plunging Eleni back into the silence of the shadowed trail.

She stood rooted to the spot, struggling to breathe. She grabbed at the crucifix, slid to her knees, and bowed to the ground, her whole body shaking.

Minutes passed. The night became colder, darker. Eleni sat up and pulled the hood of her sweatshirt over her head. Fighting through waves of panic, she faced reality. She would call the clinic first thing in the morning. No other options remained.

Decision made, she wiped her face with the edge of her sleeve and raised herself to an upright position. Her legs felt weak, like she had dragged her body through miles of rough terrain. She staggered a few steps, noticing a dark, square shape in the distance. She pointed her cell phone light at the object, walked a few steps, reached her arms forward, and grabbed the corners of the community bulletin board to steady herself. Her cell phone slid to the ground, flashing on the words of a glossy poster on the way down: "Discover the spark of the divine in every life."

She leaned into the rough wood, slid her hands to her belly, and mourned the loss, cried in silence for the small hands she would never hold, the warm body she would never rock, the tiny face she would never see.

In the distance, the faint notes of a song wafted on the air. Eleni turned toward the music. She longed for acceptance, understanding, the kindness of a human face. She stepped away from the community board, headed toward the sound. The chorus grew louder, the melody slicing into her despair with a power all its own.

Just as I am, without one plea,
But that thy blood, was shed for me.
And that thou bidd'st me come to Thee,
Oh, Lamb of God, I come, I come.[1]

Eleni hastened her step. At the end of the trail, the lights of the outdoor amphitheater beckoned.

* * * * *

Alice Jones examined the participant card on the bottom of the pile and compared the name Bob Maggiano with the white paper pictured on her cell phone. Small, tight marks. Left slant. Crowded letters. Minimal space between words. Exact match.

One weekend down. One for the kingdom.

But what of the others? Alice felt her faith slipping. She knew she should be praising God for the highly emotional man who shouted at the end of the first meeting, shook Pastor Vic's hand over and over again, eagerly received the book *Steps to Christ*, sat down on the stone bench, and strained to read the little volume as the amphitheater lights dimmed.

But she worried about the others. The initiator of the questions. The desperate young woman. Where were they? There were only two weekends left.

Alice shuffled the deck of participant cards. Opened her mouth with an airy sigh. Allowed herself the luxury of slipping into the comfortable role of Alice the worrier.

In the front of the amphitheater, Pastor Vic straightened

his things. Bob Maggiano lingered, holding *Steps to Christ* in one hand and pushing on the bench in some type of arm stretch with the other. Time to call it a night.

Alice stepped out of the lighted arena toward the small parking area behind the patch of woods. Five paces down the trail, she came to a dead stop. She could clearly hear the sound of footsteps approaching in the dark. Would Pastor Vic hear her if she called out? She slid to the side of the trail. Stayed as still as possible.

A young woman emerged from the woods, a large bulky sweatshirt covering her form. Her dark hair was pulled into a ponytail, revealing a face smeared in dirt. She trained the light of her cell phone on the path, stepping into the tiny field of white leading her forward.

Suddenly Alice felt her heart begin to pound. Standing in the shadow of a live oak, she knew. She had walked this path before. The journey toward hope. The measured steps that threatened every ounce of strength in your body. The overwhelming darkness. The tiny light.

She stepped out from behind the tree and rushed toward the girl, her arms extended. Eleni fell forward, gripped her in a tight embrace as if her whole life had waited for this moment.

"I'm Alice," she said finally. "I've been waiting for you. Let's go home."

---

1. Charlotte Elliot, "Just As I Am, Without One Plea" (1841).

Sixteen

*C*ameron Stanton strode up and down the parking lot, desperately trying to put the pieces of his life together. His business was crashing. Weston Reese called every day, hinting that his delay in joining the merger was costing him his profit. He'd barely seen Marilyn for weeks. His email was flooded with memos from Jay's teachers reporting that his son's latest pastime was skipping classes.

Why did life have to be so complicated? Even an evening on the Sun Odyssey offered no respite. The last time he had taken the vessel out, he'd had engine trouble. He spent the night floating around the bay, pacing up and down the deck, trying to troubleshoot the problem.

Cameron grabbed his briefcase and elbowed his way past the gaggle of teenagers streaming out the front door of Rollins Academy. Shouldn't Marilyn be handling this?

And wasn't Jay supposed to be the model student? His kid was nothing like these punks, tattoos spilling down their arms, hair dyed blue and pink, earbuds blocking out the world. Not even an excuse-me when they bumped into you.

Inside the building, Cameron twisted his head around in confusion. In the three years Jay had attended Rollins Academy, he'd never set foot on the campus. How did anybody make sense of the place? Hallways veered in every direction. Teachers and students rushed past, not even bothering to look Cameron's way.

Finally, he spotted a small directory on the wall that said "Guidance counselor, C-5." He studied the map then headed for the hall that constituted his best guess. Three wrong turns later, he arrived in the C-wing. Out of breath. Out of time. Out of patience.

Jay was seated at the end of a long table, flanked by a woman with long crochet braids and a middle-aged man with a buzzed head. If Cameron had expected his son to be somber, he was badly mistaken. Jay chatted amiably with the adults, who kept nodding their heads in agreement.

Cameron fought with his thoughts. Shouldn't he be relieved to see his son at ease, appearing like the old Jay, the carefree young man who had thrown a football around with him on Sunday afternoons before the accident that shattered his life? Yet here he was, summoned to the school because Jay was skipping classes for the first time in his academic career, and the boy was making a party out of the whole thing. Nothing made sense anymore.

Cameron took an empty seat near the middle of the table.

Jay stopped talking and flashed him a grateful look. The woman stood, extending her hand with a warm smile. "I'm Mrs. Ladd, the guidance counselor. This is Mr. Emory, your son's algebra II teacher. I think we're pretty close to getting this thing resolved."

"Your son's an impressive young man." Mr. Emory swiveled in his seat. "I've agreed to let him make up the classes by passing in all the missed work and sitting for two rounds of detention. That should get him up to speed and check all the boxes for complying with the behavior policy of the school."

Everything was resolved? Then why did they need him here? Didn't anyone value his time?

Cameron opened his mouth to speak, then stopped when he saw Jay's face. "It'll never happen again, Dad. I promise. I needed some time. Everything's OK now. I know where Christina is."

Cameron's heart skipped a beat as he repeated Jay's words in his mind. *I know where Christina is.* He studied the conviction in Jay's eyes. Had his son managed to discover for himself what his own father had failed to provide?

Mrs. Ladd stood. "Do you have any questions, Mr. Stanton?"

"Questions?" Cameron struggled to formulate a response.

Mr. Emory pushed a white form across the table. "If you're in agreement with the plan, just sign at the bottom below your son's name."

Cameron took the pen. Scrawled his signature.

Mr. Emory retrieved the form, slid it into his briefcase

and led the way to the door. "Thank you so much for your time, Mr. Stanton. I'm sure we can expect to find Jay back on the honor roll this semester."

"You know," Mrs. Ladd added, "nothing is scheduled in this room for the rest of the afternoon. Feel free to take the time you need to talk."

The door clicked closed. Father and son regarded each other intently. Finally, Jay broke the silence.

"I found a Bible in the library, Dad. I've been using the concordance, looking up texts."

Texts? Concordance? Cameron rolled the pen between his fingers, wrestling with his thoughts. He leaned closer to his son. "I want to hear what you found, Jay, but I have a few things to say first."

"I'm really sorry, Dad. I know I shouldn't have let my grades slip . . ."

"That's not it, Jay. Hear me out. Before your mother and I got married, we had a conversation about religion. I grew up in a churchgoing family. She did not. It was important to your mother that we shield you from any religious influences in your growing-up years. She thought teaching kids about religion was a form of brainwashing. So we took Christ out of Christmas, never taught you to pray, prevented you from hearing anything at all about the spiritual side of life."

Jay nodded slowly, his face somber.

"After our conversation about Christina a few weeks ago, I started thinking seriously about our decision, about going along with your mother, even though it made me uncomfortable. It was wrong, Jay. I was trying to keep the peace—have been trying keep the peace for years—and by doing that I robbed you of the most meaningful thing I could have ever given you. I owe you an apology."

Jay reached toward his father, placed a hand on his arm. "You did the best you could, Dad. I don't hold anything against you. We can start now. It's not too late."

Start now. Never too late. A myriad of thoughts raced through Cameron's mind.

He could think for himself. Make his own decisions. Listen to his conscience. Do what was right. Release the power others had over him. Let the chips fall where they may.

Start now. Never too late. Cameron took a deep breath. His questions, his long list of complicated questions written on the Sun Odyssey, boiled down to one basic question. And his son had just helped him answer it.

"I want to hear what you found, Jay. I want to know where Christina is right now. If we will ever get to see her again. Can we take some time this weekend? Get out a Bible? Look at some texts?"

"I would really like that, Dad. What do you have in mind? Where can we go?"

Cameron met his son's gaze squarely. "We don't have to go anywhere, Jay. We can study at home. At our own kitchen table. In broad daylight. Right smack in the middle of the house."

Seventeen

Alice Jones tiptoed into the kitchen, not wanting to awaken the young woman sleeping in the guest room. She hummed as she selected her tea from the bamboo box, dunked the peach tea bag in the steaming water with a grin on her face that was broader than the morning sun. If you had told her she would find joy again after losing Lance, she would have referred you to the nearest psychiatrist. But here she was. Eleni comfortably resting in the bigger of the two guest rooms. The other one would be fixed into a nursery.

"The Lord works in mysterious ways," she told the African violet plant on the sill. "His wonders to perform."

Alice opened her journal and reviewed her notes on Revelation's first two angels.

Give glory to God for the judgment. His perfect sacrifice is enough.

Worship the Creator. Honor Him on the seventh day.
Babylon will fall. Keep a sharp eye. Don't be deceived by
truth mixed with error.

Time to delve into the third angel's message. Alice opened
her Bible to Revelation 14, yellow highlighter in hand, ready
to get to work. Beginning with verse 9, she made her way
through the passage.

Then a third angel followed them, saying with a loud
voice, "If anyone worships the beast and his image,
and receives his mark on his forehead or on his hand,
he himself shall also drink of the wine of the wrath of
God, which is poured out full strength into the cup of
His indignation. He shall be tormented with fire and
brimstone in the presence of the holy angels and in the
presence of the Lamb. And the smoke of their torment
ascends forever and ever; and they have no rest day or
night, who worship the beast and his image, and whoever
receives the mark of his name."

Here is the patience of the saints; here are those who
keep the commandments of God and the faith of Jesus
(Revelation 14:9–12).

Serious stuff. Alice highlighted the phrases *beast and his
image* and *mark on his forehead or on his hand.* Then she
scanned through the rest of the text, settling on the last
verse: "Here is the patience of the saints; here are those who
keep the commandments of God and the faith of Jesus."
She put the yellow marker down, selected a blue one, and

highlighted the whole last sentence. That was definitely the group she wanted to be in. Patient saints full of faith.

Two groups, she added to her journal. *Don't give in to the beast. Be patient. Keep the commandments. Have the faith of Jesus.*

Alice stirred her tea. The third angel's message wasn't hard to understand after you figured out the second angel's message. She remembered the contrast between the people who bowed down to Nebuchadnezzar's golden image and the three Hebrew boys who refused to follow the crowd. Same as what was ahead. One group of people would follow all of God's commandments. The other would not. It was as simple as that.

Mark on forehead, she wrote in her journal. *Symbol for* thinking *apart from God's law. Mark on hand. Symbol for* acting *apart from God's law.*

Alice powered up her tablet. The words in Revelation described what was coming. No reason to doubt the third angel's words. So far, everything in Daniel and Revelation matched up perfectly with Earth's history. Even Google could tell you the story. She typed in the words *conquest of Babylon.*

In 539 B.C., less than a century after the founding of the Neo-Babylonian Empire, the legendary Persian king Cyrus the Great conquered it. The fall of Babylon was complete when the empire came under Persian control.[1]

The fall of Babylon. And then the other kingdoms, one after the other. Persia, Greece, and finally Rome. That's where things got really interesting.

Alice remembered googling the number of countries in the world and finding the answer: 193 countries plus Palestine and the Holy See. The Holy See? That was an interesting phenomenon. The only country in the world that had nothing to do with geography. Alice typed the phrase into the browser and studied the first article that popped up:

"The apostolic see of Diocese of Rome was established in the 1st century by Saint Peter and Saint Paul, then the capital of the Roman Empire, according to Catholic tradition. The legal status of the Catholic Church and its property was recognized by the Edict of Milan in 313 by Roman emperor Constantine the Great, and it became the state church of the Roman Empire by the Edict of Thessalonica in 380 by Emperor Theodosius I."[2]

Alice took a slow slip of her peach tea. If you doubted the Bible, all you had to do was open a history book. The prophecies did not get it wrong. Only one country in the world stood out from the others as a religious-political organization. The Holy See. She remembered studying about Emperor Constantine moving the capital to the eastern side of his empire. That left a vacuum. Rome needed a ruler, and Constantine gave the role to the bishop of Rome. Fast-forward a few centuries and the bishop was claiming power over all the other bishops. And he had a new title: pope, the Latin word for "father."

Alice shook her head. It was hard to believe the Holy See was still listed as a separate country, added to the 193 others. The mix of church and state. That's where everything was going to become really threatening.

She gathered a few Bible commentaries and continued studying. The seventh-day Sabbath would be the final test of loyalty. That was clear. She found it interesting how everything traced back to Constantine. The same guy who gave the Catholic Church its legal status as a religious-political entity also had a big part in changing the day of worship.

She typed the name Constantine and the words *day of rest* into the search bar. Reading a number of articles, she could come to only one conclusion. Mixing truth with error was a dangerous thing—a really dangerous thing.

Alice shook her head. Constantine did a lot to defend the Christian faith. That was for sure. But he also took it on himself to change God's seventh-day Sabbath to the first day of the week. And somehow, he got away with it! *Even the authors of the articles I'm reading seem to be missing the point,* she thought as she read one in particular, which stated, "The gradual process towards Christian tradition and ritual was underscored in 321, when, on the 7th of March, Constantine decreed that dies Solis, or 'the day of the sun,' should be observed as a universal day of rest. The pious observance of the Sabbath was important in expressing thanks for God's toil. Previously all Christians worshiped on Saturday, the seventh day of the week."[3]

Well, she wasn't going to let any emperor, pastor, priest, king, president, or world leader get her to break God's commandments! She would keep the Sabbath as it came from God's own hand—on the seventh day as a reminder of His mighty power in creating the world. She added a final note to her journal: *The seventh-day Sabbath. Seal of loyalty to God.*

"Alice?" Eleni entered the room, rubbing the sleep from her eyes. "Did you ever find out who pinned that list of questions to the community board? I've been thinking. If Bob were the one who wrote the question before mine, he might have been the one who tacked the note to the board. That means he must know something."

"Good morning yourself!" Alice crossed the tiled floor and gave Eleni a warm embrace. "Wonderful idea. I've been concerned that we have only one weekend left to find the mysterious note-writer. If he doesn't show up next week, I don't know how we'll ever find him. The guy just seems so troubled. I feel such a strong burden to share God's truth with him. After all, he's the one who started the whole thing. If it weren't for him, you and I would not be together now."

"I don't even want to think about that. I was at the end, Alice. Just about ready to extinguish the spark of the divine."

Alice the warrior lifted her head. "You're here now. Safe. We've got two of the three note-writers on the right path. Pastor Vic tells me Bob is devouring the book *Steps to Christ* like a teenager who hasn't eaten in a week. We have to believe that the Holy Spirit is working in the lives of all of you. Let's pray that He'll lead us to the last of the three searching souls."

---

1. "Babylon," History, updated July 13, 2022, https://www.history.com/topics/ancient-middle-east/babylonia.

2. Wikipedia, s.v. "Holy See," updated November 16, 2022, https://en.wikipedia.org/wiki/Holy_See.

3. "Constantine Decrees 'Sun-Day' as Day of Rest Instead of Saturday in Year 321," Facts and History, accessed November 21, 2022, https://factsandhistory.com/constantine-decrees-sun-day-as-day-of-rest-instead-of-saturday-on-march-7-321/.

Eighteen

Cameron Stanton arose early, brewed a pot of coffee, and removed everything from the mahogany chest in the living room. At the very bottom, under a pile of blankets, he found his Bible. Holding the Book in his hands, he felt something awaken inside him, a sense of hope and freedom he hadn't experienced in years. He opened the small Bible to the second page. He read the inscription: "To Cameron on your tenth birthday. Love, Mom and Dad."

It's been a long time, Mom and Dad, but I'm back. I'm not sure where you are. If you can see me in my own living room, holding this Bible like something off the black market, you must be wondering what got into me. I guess I'm wondering that too.

The front door opened abruptly, and Marilyn entered the room in her jogging suit. She stared at the black book in her husband's hands for one long, hard second. "I've seen this coming, Cameron. I need some time. I've rented a temporary apartment downtown. I'll be leaving later this morning."

Cameron nodded, suddenly aware that he had lost Marilyn a long time ago, that he had never been the person she wanted him to be. "This is who I am," he said quietly. "I'll be here, Marilyn. Waiting for you to come back."

She paused, opened her mouth as if to say something, then left the room.

* * * * *

Jay awoke on Saturday morning to the sun streaming through the blinds. He checked his cell phone and saw that it was 10:30. He was an hour late. He threw on an old pair of jeans and a faded T-shirt and headed downstairs.

"I was wondering what happened to you," his father greeted him in the kitchen. "I guess you needed a little extra rest. I've got some blueberry muffins here."

Two pens, a notebook, and a small Bible waited on the table.

"Thanks, Dad. Give me a minute to grab a few things. I can't wait to show you what I've found."

He pounded up the stairs and back down again, reappearing in the kitchen with the library Bible, a stack of index cards, and his notebook. He took a large bite of a muffin, gulped down a swallow of milk, and opened the Bible.

"The first thing I looked up was the word *soul*. And it's not what you think it is."

Cameron watched in amazement as his son navigated the pages in the Bible like he'd been doing it all his life.

"The first place you start is right here in Genesis. The Bible says that when God made man He breathed into his nostrils and man became a living soul. What does that tell you, Dad?"

"That man wasn't alive before God breathed into his nostrils?"

"Right. And what did it take to make a human being? Two things."

"I guess that would be the body God made for Adam and the breath He breathed into it."

"Exactly. So, what's a soul?"

"Body and breath."

"Check. One down. A soul is not some weird thing floating around in the cosmos. It's a complete person. Period."

"Interesting." Jay made it all so logical. How had he missed it all these years? "That means Christina is not a soul floating around somewhere, half dead, half alive. If that's the case, where is she?"

"We are almost getting to the good part. Hold on, Dad. Wait until you read these texts. You're going to be blown away."

Jay thumbed through his Bible, stopping somewhere around the middle. "I'm not exactly sure how you pronounce this book, but when the concordance led me to E-c-c-l-e-s-i-a-s-t-e-s, chapter nine, verse five, I felt like I had taken a bullet right between the eyes. All hope drained out of me."

Cameron studied his son. If the Bible offered good news, why this? "Go ahead and read it out loud, Dad."

Cameron cleared his throat and read aloud:

For the living know that they will die;
But the dead know nothing,
And they have no more reward,
For the memory of them is forgotten.

Cameron shook his head. "She's gone. Just gone. Not in heaven. Not in hell. Just gone. Then why have I been led to believe all these years that you go to heaven when you die? Or, worse, to hell?"

Cameron hesitated, wrestling with his thoughts. It wasn't just Christina who was gone. It was his parents, his grand-parents, the foreman at the plant who'd had a sudden heart attack and left three children behind.

Jay leaned forward, his dark eyes intense. "But not gone forever, Dad. She's resting. She's spared the anguish of knowing her parents split. She didn't have to watch me cry myself to sleep every night for a year. She has no idea her favorite teacher has cancer and her best friend dropped out of school and can barely afford to eat."

Cameron reflected for a moment, then spoke. "I never really thought about it like that. I mean, my own parents, if they could look down and see me wrestling, agonizing with life issues . . ." He paused for a moment, then laughed. "Really, it seems ludicrous now. Like the other night, when I was floating around in the bay trying to reach your cell.

If my parents were able to look down, my mother would have been having a canary. I can see it now, 'Lloyd, do something! We can't just sit back on this cloud! That's our son down there!' "

Jay laughed. "Yeah. After I read the other texts and discovered the good news, I was relieved that Christina is just resting. There's a lot of stuff that people are better of not knowing."

He flipped ahead in the borrowed Bible. "The book of John actually compares death to a sleep. There's this whole story in chapter eleven about Jesus bringing a guy back to life." Jay stopped, looked up at his father, his eyes twinkling. "You didn't think you could keep me from hearing about Jesus all these years, did you? I mean I had a head start there. He's everywhere, even in this crazy world we live in. You can't block a kid's ears for eighteen years."

"Anyway, this guy named Lazarus died. Jesus was heading for the grave and was talking to His disciples. You know, the twelve guys that followed Him around everywhere? Anyway, moving right along, Jesus actually referred to death as a sleep. You can read it in verses eleven through fifteen."

Cameron turned to the section in his small Bible and read:

These things He said, and after that He said to them, "Our friend Lazarus sleeps, but I go that I may wake him up."

Then His disciples said, "Lord, if he sleeps he will get well." However, Jesus spoke of his death, but they thought that He was speaking about taking rest in sleep.

Then Jesus said to them plainly, "Lazarus is dead. And I am glad for your sakes that I was not there, that you may believe. Nevertheless let us go to him."

"Pretty clear, right Dad?"

"It is. I just can't get over the irony of the whole thing. You're the kid we were trying to shield from religion. And now you're explaining the Bible to me."

Jay laughed. "OK, now for the good part. Dad, keep turning in your Bible. Go a little further toward the end of the New Testament. You're going to find five books beginning with the letter *T*. They're all in alphabetical order. I want you to turn to First Thessalonians, chapter four. Start with verse thirteen and read all the way to the end, to verse eighteen."

Cameron located the book of Timothy, then paged back to 1 Thessalonians and read the passage:

But I do not want you to be ignorant, brethren, concerning those who have fallen asleep, lest you sorrow as others who have no hope. For if we believe that Jesus died and rose again, even so God will bring with Him those who sleep in Jesus.

For this we say to you by the word of the Lord, that we who are alive and remain until the coming of the Lord will by no means precede those who are asleep. For the Lord Himself will descend from heaven with a shout, with the voice of an archangel, and with the trumpet of God. And the dead in Christ will rise first. Then we who are alive and remain shall be caught up together with them in the clouds to meet the Lord in the air. And thus we shall always be with the Lord. Therefore comfort one another with these words.

"Do you get it, Dad? All those centuries ago, those words were written to encourage us here today. Christina is not going to stay in the grave forever. Through the power of Jesus, she's going to catapult out of the ground. She's going to skyrocket into heaven, Dad. Blaze through the sky with the power of Jesus. He breathed life into Adam. He pulled Lazarus out of the ground. He's going to do it for Christina, too."

Jay's face was radiant. Cameron's heart pounded. He felt like he was sitting in an old-time revival meeting and his son just put Billy Graham to shame.

Jay paused then said in a low voice, "But there's one more thing, Dad. Now that I've figured all that out, I have another question. What's up with the texts in Luke that talk about Jesus' death and resurrection? They mention something about His body resting in the tomb over the Sabbath, and Sabbath means 'day of rest.' And if you put the texts together, it's clearly talking about Saturday, the seventh day of the week. I spent a little time looking, but I can't find anything in the Bible about God changing the Sabbath to Sunday. Apparently, all these churches around here know something I don't. Who can we talk to about that?"

Nineteen

Bob Maggiano repeated the words for the third time. "There's really not much to say. If you insist on seeing where I found the note, I will show you. But it was just wedged into a clump of beach grass. I can't see how that is going to lead you to the originator of the questions."

Alice stood firm. "This afternoon. As soon as you get out of work, meet me at the park."

Bob wrapped up at the office by 4:15 P.M., rushed home, changed into his running clothes, and blew into the park at 4:38 P.M. He checked his watch. Not even close to a four-minute mile. But who ever said he had to be perfect?

Alice waited by the bulletin board, all business. She pointed to the pitted paper, the green letters still visible. "Looks like there's dried salt on here. Maybe that's a clue."

"I hate to burst your bubble, Alice. But we live beside the

bay. There's salt on everything. Let's go. I need to get this over with. Pastor Vic is coming to study the Bible with me in less than an hour."

Bob took off, heading toward Maritime Drive. "Funny thing," he said, passing Alice's house. "I used to see you out here waving at me when I ran past. I thought you were crazy."

"I'm still crazy enough not to give up on God's children," Alice said. "Now, where did you find that note?"

Bob picked up the pace. "We'll get there, Alice. The question is, Can you keep up with me?"

Halfway down the hill he stopped. "Right there. I remember the clump of grass because it was set apart from the others. Planted in its own space."

Alice caught her breath. The tall wheat was beautiful. Each seed dazzled red-gold in the setting sun. "Thank you," she said. "Somehow I have to believe God is going to bring us all together."

* * * * *

Alice tapped the pastor's number one more time. Why wouldn't he pick up? She wanted to have faith. She really did. But this new piece of news had her pacing up and down the living room like a caged animal.

"Expect heavy rainfall to begin at around six o'clock this evening, continuing throughout the weekend. Wind gusts will pick up at midnight, with tropical conditions for the north side of the bay arriving by early morning."

Alice moved past the flat-screen TV for the hundredth time, noting the intensity on the newscaster's face. How would they continue the meetings? They couldn't expect people to sit in the amphitheater, umbrellas blowing inside out while Pastor Vic brought them up to speed on the third angel's message. And if they didn't meet in the amphitheater, that wiped out the last chance for the original note-writer to even find them. What if he had already walked past the board? What if he was planning, even now, to join them?

Alice sucked in her breath. She wanted to be Alice the warrior. She really did. But there was so much more to worry about now. What if Eleni had trouble coming home from work? What if she slipped and fell on her way to the car? What if something happened to the baby?

She tapped Pastor Vic's number one more time. *Answer the phone, pastor. We need to come up with a plan.*

Alice continued pacing. Walked through the living room. Down the hall. Into the family room. Out through the kitchen. She could almost picture the note-writer. Sitting at a desk somewhere. Feeling pressure from work. Pressure from home. Desperately writing the questions. Then panicking. Afraid to disrupt the status quo. Afraid the note might be read by somebody at work. Afraid his family might find it. Crumpling up the paper. Tossing it out as he walked toward Oyster Bay. Missing the trash can.

And then the worst part. Alice pictured him sauntering through the park. Maybe he would have a meeting at the library. He'd sit in the back row. Try not to ask too many questions. He'd get up halfway through the presentation.

Need air. Maybe even a smoke. He'd walk around a bit. Notice the bulletin board. Absentmindedly read the notices that read "Fall mullet run, "Fishing contest, "Seaside School fall festival." Then his eyes would widen as he spotted his own note. Heart in his throat, he'd spy the flyer and read the teasers Alice had formulated: "Find out what will happen to your personal freedoms in the days ahead. Learn why it's important to listen to your conscience. Hear why scientists believe in intelligent design."

He'd make a point, then and there, to show up at the amphitheater for the next meeting. A little bit of hope would enter his heart. Alice could almost see his face. The slight softening of the eyes. The straightening of the shoulders. He'd go back to his meeting in the library with a new spring in his steps.

And then . . .

Alice's cell phone buzzed. She jammed it to her ear. Didn't even wait for the pastor to identify himself.

"Pastor Vic? Have you heard the news? We're in trouble."

How could the man be so calm? Change the meeting to the church? But how would the original note-writer ever find them? Faith? The God who brought Bob and Eleni to the truth was not finished yet?

Men of the cloth could be maddening sometimes! A plan. They needed a plan. At 7:00 P.M. on Saturday and Sunday nights, the meetings would continue at the church.

God would take care of the rest.

Slipping the cell phone into her hand-sewn pouch, Alice the worrier couldn't help but decide to give God a little help. There was still time. Maybe the original note-writer would stroll through the park tonight.

She grabbed a flyer and a permanent marker.

> *Location changed. Northside Seventh-day Adventist Church. Corner of Spring and Meadows Drive.*

Leaving a note for Eleni, she rushed out of the house. The first gusts of wind were already beginning to sweep into the area. Overhead, the sky darkened. A bank of dark gray clouds raced past a lighter set of mouse-colored wisps. The tops of palm trees rippled. Alice prayed, "Lord, hold off the storm. Let me get this posted. Send the note-writer sooner rather than later."

At the board, she quickly removed the old flyer and placed the new one close to the center. She inserted the tacks and put up her hood just as the first few drops of rain made their staccato taps on the walk.

She arrived home soaked to the skin, visualizing a lone figure clad in a trench coat, pointing a flashlight to the corkboard.

Twenty

While the people of Northside slept, a mighty wind blew in from the bay. Dinghies crashed together, oarlocks clanging. Mountains of waves blasted sand from the beach. Tree branches and palm fronds rolled across yards and into the streets.

At the park, swings whipped upward, wrapping themselves around the top beam.

Torrents of rain soaked picnic tables and created a deepening puddle under the slide. The sky sent a cinematic roll of flashing light into deep, purplish darkness.

Just after midnight, a large gust roared toward the community bulletin board, tearing a tattered sheet of paper from the cork. The white note flew upward, disintegrated, dissolved, and settled into a thousand disparate molecules in the bottom of the bay.

Cameron Stanton awakened in an empty room to the sound of rain pounding on the roof and waves roaring in the distance. Opening the shades, he surveyed the scene outside the window. Broken tree branches littered the yard. The flag on the corner of the property flapped wildly. Rivulets of water coursed down the sidewalks. Not a good day for a Saturday morning drive.

"Up for a Bible study?" Jay popped into the room in his pajama shorts. "I've been up half the night. I've got some texts for us to look at."

"I can't think of a better way to ride out a tropical storm."

Downstairs the two settled into the kitchen. Cameron started a pot of coffee. Jay scrounged around in the refrigerator, found a couple of cheese sticks, and turned to his father.

"It took me until after midnight to realize I just wasn't going to find anything in the Bible about the change of the Sabbath. God Himself kept the first Sabbath after creating the earth. He reminded us to remember the Sabbath in the fourth commandment. The people kept it in the Old Testament. They kept it in the New Testament."

The boy actually sounded like preacher material. How had he raised this kid?

Cameron chuckled. "Just give me the texts one at a time."

"Well, we can start with Creation week. Back to my favorite book. The easiest one to find. Take a look at Genesis, chapter two, and read the first three verses."

Cameron opened the small Bible. "Thus the heavens and the earth, and all the host of them, were finished. And on the seventh day God ended His work which He had done, and He rested on the seventh day from all His work which He had done. Then God blessed the seventh day and sanctified it, because in it He rested from all His work which God had created and made."

"Can't get any clearer than that, can you?"

"I guess not. What else do you have for me?"

"Let's read the fourth commandment. You'll find that in Exodus, chapter twenty, verses eight through eleven. Just one book of the Bible away."

"Got it," said Cameron. "It says, 'Remember the Sabbath day, to keep it holy. Six days you shall labor and do all your work, but the seventh day is the Sabbath of the LORD your God. In it you shall do no work: you, nor your son, nor your daughter, nor your male servant, nor your female servant, nor your cattle, nor your stranger who is within your gates. For in six days the LORD made the heavens and the earth, the sea, and all that is in them, and rested the seventh day. Therefore the LORD blessed the Sabbath day and hallowed it.' "

"It's right there. With all the other commandments. Do you think any of those have been changed, Dad? Is it OK for me to commit murder or steal your car?"

"Don't even think about it."

"Then why would God pick out one commandment and change it? I mean, He wrote the commandments with His own finger."

"True. You have a way of boiling everything down. Making everything so obvious. Makes me wonder how I missed it in the first place. What else do you have for me?"

"Let me tell you about a couple of other places in the Bible. Remember when the Israelites were out in the desert with nothing to eat? God sent them this food from the sky called manna. But they could gather enough for only one day. I guess this showed their faith. If they cheated and tried to scoop up more, the stuff went rank the next day. But there was one exception. Can you guess what day that was?"

"If I'm following you correctly, I'm going to vote for Friday. They probably got enough so they didn't have to work on the seventh-day Sabbath."

"Nailed it. You're actually a pretty good student, Dad."

"You think I'm good? You should see my son. When he actually does show up to class, he can blow the others away."

"Very funny, Dad. Convinced that the Sabbath was kept in the Old Testament? Ready to move on to the New?"

"Go for it."

"Check out Luke, chapter four, verse sixteen."

"Give me a minute. Got to get over to the New Testament. I'm starting to remember my way around this old Bible. Matthew, Mark, Luke . . . here it is. It says, 'So He came to Nazareth, where He had been brought up. And as His custom was, He went into the synagogue on the Sabbath day, and stood up to read.' "

"We're talking about Jesus here. His custom was to keep the Sabbath."

"Pretty clear there. I'd like to read the passage you were telling me about the other day. The verses that got you questioning the whole first-day-of-the-week thing in the first place. When Jesus was in the tomb. Where did you find that?"

"I'll read it for you. You'll find it in Luke. I started reading the end of chapter twenty-three and then continued into chapter twenty-four. It's all there. Laid out as plain as day. I was like, 'Am I missing something here?' I read it three times the day before I was called into the guidance office."

"Ah. Another reason you were failing algebra. Skipping classes *and* pulling all-nighters."

"All for a good cause, Dad. All for a good cause. The passage I'm about to read starts by talking about this guy named Joseph, but not the father of Jesus. This was some rich guy who dared to buck the system. He was ticked about what happened to Jesus. So he waited around. Wanted to at least give Him a decent burial. Then he took the body of Jesus and brought it to a tomb carved in the rock. Now listen to the sequence of events here."

Jay opened his borrowed Bible to the passage and read it aloud:

Then he took it down, wrapped it in linen, and laid it in a tomb that was hewn out of the rock, where no one had ever lain before. That day was the Preparation, and the Sabbath drew near.

And the women who had come with Him from Galilee followed after, and they observed the tomb and how His body was laid. Then they returned and prepared spices and fragrant oils. And they rested on the Sabbath according to the commandment (Luke 23:53–56).

"You following so far? First came the preparation day. Then came the Sabbath day. Now watch this. Chapter twenty-four, verse one, says, 'Now on the first day of the week, very early in the morning, they, and certain other women with them, came to the tomb bringing the spices which they had prepared.'

"So if the women came to the tomb on the first day of the week, after resting on the Sabbath, what day was the Sabbath?"

"Totally clear. The seventh, Saturday."

"Nailed it again! It's so obvious, even a guy like you can figure it out."

"Thanks for the compliment. Look, Jay. We've got to find a group that knows about all this. We can't be the only ones."

Twenty-One

Alice Jones sat in the mothers room in the back of the church, one eye on the open door leading to the foyer, the other on the glass overlooking the sanctuary. This was the perfect spot, she decided as she peered at Eleni, who was front and center, furiously taking notes. Through the speaker on the wall Alice could hear Pastor Vic laying out all the details of the third angel's message. "Now is the time to commit to keeping all of God's commandments. It may seem like the whole world is against you. The pressure will be high. But keep your faith in the One who gave His all for you . . ."

Outside the window, wet tree branches glistened in the parking lot. Alice adjusted her weight in the small chair. At least the storm had died down at noon. Praise the Lord, the regulars had all managed to come out.

What a faith journey! Alice's mind replayed the script that had landed all of them in this place at this time. The whole thing was beyond belief. The note. The flyer. The outdoor amphitheater. Bob Maggiano jumping up and shouting hallelujah. Eleni making her way through the dark by the light of a cell phone.

But what about the guy who started it all? Analyzing the handwriting, Alice had determined it was a male. Boxy letters. Male handwriting. No question about it. Would they ever know who he was?

For some reason, Alice could not get the man out of her mind. The questions were so genuine, so honest. What happens when you surrender your freedom? Can you be truly happy when you silence your own conscience? How much money is enough? Who is responsible for the happiness of the family? Which comes first: Obligations to others or living up to beliefs?

The guy needed to hear about the three angels' messages! Why couldn't he just show up? Alice rehearsed her summary notes in her head.

Angel one:

1. *Give glory to God for the judgment. His perfect sacrifice is enough.*

2. *Worship the Creator. Honor Him on the seventh day.*

Angel two:

3. *Babylon will fall. Keep a sharp eye. Don't be deceived by truth mixed with error.*

Angel three:

4. *Political-religious leaders will enforce worship on the*

first day. Continue to keep the seventh-day Sabbath. Stay patient and anchor your faith in Jesus.

It was all so clear. And now the meetings were wrapping up, and her plan was becoming part of history. The opportunity to find the original note-writer was slim.

In the sanctuary, Pastor Vic pleaded earnestly with the congregation. "Never, ever surrender your freedom to an individual or any group, be it small or large. God's government is one of freedom, not force. No one—not a church, not a government organization, not even your own family—has the right to pressure you into doing something you know is wrong."

Pastor Vic was doing such a good job. It had taken a little bit for him to catch the vision, but now that he'd climbed on board, he was knocking it out of the park. The three angels' messages, answering the cries of people's hearts. Right here. Right now.

Exactly what the note-writer needed to hear.

Alice could barely take it. Maybe she would stop by the park and grab the original note in the morning. See if there was anything at all on the paper that might give her a clue. One more night. They needed to find him.

The paper? How could it have survived the storm? By now it was probably just a few soaked scraps hanging on to the tack. But God used just one small loaf and five fishes to feed a crowd.

"Oh, Lord," Alice prayed as she bowed her head. "You have to help me. I know I should have faith, but sometimes I get confused about where my part stops and Your part takes over. I want to help You. I want to do Your will. But sometimes it seems like I don't think You can work unless I am in the middle of it. I surrender this whole thing to You. You know the name of the note-writer. You know where he lives. You even know the number of hairs on his head . . ."

From the parking lot, a car door slammed. Then another.

Alice lifted her head. Looked out the window. A dark-haired young man was heading toward the church. An older man walked behind him.

* * * * *

"I really didn't expect to see cars in the parking lot at this time of night." Cameron caught up with Jay by the stairs to the church. "According to their website, they meet on Saturday mornings. Services are at nine o'clock and eleven o'clock. Not sure what's going on here tonight."

"I guess we're about to find out, Dad." Jay swung open the door to the foyer, revealing a warm, red-carpeted room. He headed for a wooden rack on the wall filled with pamphlets and stuffed three in his pocket. *Can Dead People Talk? Myths About Hell. When Freedom Dies.* "Looks like we're on the right track."

From the sanctuary, the preacher's words floated into the foyer. "God has a plan for each of our lives. He knows your needs, your wants, the deepest questions of your heart. And if you let Him, He will lead you to Him."

"Amen," said a voice from the far corner of the foyer. A smiling woman rushed toward them. Grabbed their hands.

Shook them like they had just reappeared on the planet after a long absence. "I'm Alice," she said. "We've been waiting for you."